Christmas and Cannolis

by

Peggy Jaeger

Christmas and Cannolis

Cover Art by *Debbie Taylor*

The Wild Rose Press, Inc.
PO Box 708
Adams Basin, NY 14410-0708
Visit us at www.thewildrosepress.com

Publishing History
First Champagne Rose Edition, 2018
Print ISBN 978-1-5092-2181-3
Digital ISBN 978-1-5092-2182-0

Published in the United States of America

Dedication

To all the bakers I know. You understand what it means
to add a cup of love to everything you bake.

It had been a long, long time since a guy's hands had been on me in anything resembling a carnal way. My ex had decamped to parts unknown five years ago after signing the divorce papers, and I'd been so busy rebuilding my life that adding any kind of relationship to it wasn't even a notion.

Besides, with my hovering parents, one of whom worked for me while the other popped in daily to check up on their only daughter, I had enough on my plate fending off the men they wanted to introduce me to. Guys who, for the most part, had shady lifestyles, carried concealed, and owed my father innumerable favors. And by favors, I mean the kind that usually get signed for in blood and paid back the same way.

Welcome to *mia famiglia*.

Chapter 1

Regina's tips for surviving in a big Italian family:
1. Ignore behavior that will never change.

"Regina Maria, get down here. A guy wants to see th'owner."

My mother's loud, shrill voice exploded up the bakery's staircase to my office, pulling me out of my monthly receipts review. I winced from the piercing shriek neighborhood dogs had been known to cower from and pressed the intercom on my desk phone that connected to the front of the bakery. "I'll be right there, Ma."

I didn't bother telling her she should use the intercom and not resort to screeching like a *vecchia strega*—an old witch—if she needed something. After three years of working for me at the bakery and a lifetime spent listening to her interact with others, I'd come to realize it was a lost cause trying to change a behavior that was ingrained in her DNA.

I did a quick swipe through my unruly hair to make sure it was still secure in its ponytail and ran a hand down the front of my apron. I'd been up since three a.m. baking, and before going into my office I'd been covered from chin to knees in white streaks. I looked like I'd been slashed by a homicidal pastry chef wielding a flour-coated knife. With my order book in my hands, I jogged down the stairs.

Since opening my own bakery, Angie's, made possible with a loan from my father—and by loan, I mean the kind you don't pay back with interest that only an Italian father with lots of connections can grant—I'd been busy seven days a week, sixteen hours a day. Running your own business is a fulltime job that never allows a day off, never allows a respite from the chaos. My life, literally, is my business. I even live above the bakery in a rent-free apartment courtesy—again—of my father, so I was never far from home or work. Sometimes I'd go a week without even venturing beyond my storefront.

Pathetic? Yeah, maybe just a smidge.

"I stuck him at a corner table and gave him a cuppa coffee and a cookie," my mother told me when she spied me. At a spit above five foot, Ursula, my sixty-eight-year-old mother, is as round as she is tall, but blessed with more vitality than that battery-powered bunny who's super energized. The fact that she drinks a gallon of espresso a day—straight—adds to that vivacity. Her thick childhood Brooklyn accent was still on yelling mode in order to be heard over the din in the bakery.

I kissed her plump cheek. The scent of almonds and warm sugar wafted up to me from the cookie-laden tray in her hand.

"Thanks, Ma."

"*Prego.*"

"He give you a name?"

She shrugged, the corners of her lips tugging down to her chin as her shoulders lifted up. When I'd been little, I'd thought they were connected because I never saw my mother lift her shoulders without her mouth pulling down into a frown.

"Somethin' American, I don't remember what."

This is a common facet of my mother's personality: she only remembers names that either sound, or are, Italian in origin. Everything else is relegated to "sounding American," whether it's of Chinese, Russian, or Asian extraction. The fact that a name doesn't end in a vowel renders it impossible for her to recall it.

The bakery was packed with preholiday business, the reason for the high noise level. With the crowd three deep at the register and a line running the entire length of the filled-to-busting display cases, it seemed like everyone in my little Tribeca neighborhood of Manhattan was purchasing their Thanksgiving pies, cakes, cookies, and breads today.

Not that I'm complaining. Business is brisk most days of the year, but holidays are nonstop. Hence, the three a.m. start to my day. I have a cadre of employees who work the night shift from nine until four baking daily bread, rolls, and pastry orders so I can get a little more than three hours of sleep in twenty-four. But during holidays, I get an early jump on my workday, knowing I'll be moving more goods than usual through the store.

I wove through the throng of customers all clutching little raffle-like tickets with next-in-line numbers written on them and smiled at a few familiar faces. I never tire of seeing how happy my customers look when they leave my shop with their white boxes tied with red string, filled with the day's baked goodies.

The aroma of warm yeast, caramelized sugar, and

bread baking permeated the entire place and spilled out onto the busy street beyond my front doors. Even though I had a wealth of frequent, repeat customers, I still did a good foot traffic business with people who followed their noses to my door. Once inside and able to view all the sweets, treats, and savory items I offered, a customer never left without buying something—be it a box of anisette *pizzelles* or a yard of fresh herbed bread.

I spotted my customer in the seat my mother indicated. His back was toward me, but I could tell he was tall from how much of him shot up from the chair. Since I didn't know how to address him, I simply said, "Excuse me?" when I finally arrived at the table. I was all set to introduce myself and ask how I could help him, but before the words could form in my throat I was struck mute. Truly. I stopped short, my mouth falling open like unfilled cannoli shells, and no sound came out.

He turned to me at the exact moment a slice of midday November sunlight streamed through the window, landing right on him and surrounding his head in a halo of bright, brilliant light. I wouldn't have been surprised if a choir of angels started belting out celestial high notes because the guy could have been a charter member of the Messenger of God club.

Facially, he looked a little older than my thirty-two, but not over the forty-year mark yet. Where my hair is the color of wet ink, his was a shock of silver threaded with faint stripes of peppery black above his ears. It looked so thick and touch-worthy, the tips of my fingers were actually tingling to clutch the ends and grab on. Eyes the color of threatening storm clouds—

4

gray and tinged with pale shards of blue—peered up at me, a question pulling at their corners. Eyelashes most women had to pay for framed his lids naturally. His jaw was square, his cheekbones carved from marble by a master sculptor.

But his mouth—*Madre di Dio*, his mouth. It was about as perfect as two lips meeting in the center of a face could be. Full and thick with that natural rimmed outline women were forced to create with a liner pencil, it was the most kissable mouth I'd ever seen. Tinted the color of aged Barolo—my father's favorite wine—ripe and smooth, full-bodied and intense, it simply stopped me in my tracks.

While I stood there, voiceless and paralyzed, my mind was still able to register how I wanted to sample his mouth to see if it was as tasty and satisfying as a sip of that wine.

His skin had an olive, sun-kissed hue, like my brothers', that I hoped meant he had some kind of Mediterranean history, despite a name my mother couldn't remember.

Ma's voice penetrated over the bakery's racket calling out the next number in line and pulled me out of my immobile state.

I blinked a few times and shook my head, surprised when I didn't hear rattling. While I was doing that, tall and god-like rose from the chair and put out one of his hands.

I knew I was supposed to take it, but the blood hadn't gotten back to my head yet to instruct me in how to accomplish the task. Staring down at it and then back up at him, I watched as the question in the corners of his eyes morphed into confusion.

5

I knew exactly how he felt.

"Sorry," I said, shaking my head again. I slipped my hand into his, and for the second time in less than a minute, my body went still.

The day was cold and dry, and the bakery was, as usual, stifling due to the continuous oven use so when our fingers touched a tiny spark shot off from the contact. My customer's perfect mouth pulled into a jaw-wide smile that had my knees wobbling and my toes tingling inside my work clogs.

Gesu.

"Sorry about that." I slid into the chair opposite him and pointed for him to do the same. "Dry air outside, dry in here, makes for lots of electrical sparks."

He sat and placed his hands on top of the table, bracketing the white coffee mug and plate with a half-eaten *duetto,* a butter cookie dipped in melted chocolate and hazelnuts, that heart-tripping smile still in place.

"I'm Regina," I said, looking back up at his face. "You wanted to speak with me?"

"Connor Gilhooly."

And there flew the Mediterranean ancestry thoughts right out the bakery window.

"I asked to speak to the owner."

"That would be me."

His eyes widened while he cocked his head a bit. I should have been insulted, but wasn't. It wasn't the first time someone who didn't know me doubted the truth.

"Owner. Main baker. Cookie chef. Head bottle washer when the need calls for it. Angie's is my bakery, so…"

"I'm sorry. I didn't mean to insult you—"

"You didn't."

"—but you look so…"

"Inexperienced?"

His lips pulled back up into that delicious smile. "I was going to say young, but it sounded rude when I heard it in my head."

"I'm older than I look," I said, giving him my own smile. "So why don't you tell me what you need?" Was it wrong of me to wish he'd say, "You?"

"I'm in kind of a bind."

A phrase I was familiar with since I'd heard it often when I still lived at home, usually in the middle of the night from one of Pop's frantic "friends" when he picked up a ringing phone.

"Oh?"

"Yeah, well"—he scrubbed his hands through the hair at his temples, *lucky hands*—"my assistant had to go out early on maternity leave two weeks ago, and since she's been gone, I've been putting out administrative fires and trying to play catch-up."

I nodded for him to continue.

"Every year I throw a big holiday party for a charity I support. We had a venue booked, the food all ordered, then the place where it was going to be held went into Chapter 11 receivership last week. Closed down, with no way to get in touch with the owners."

"Ouch."

I felt the air from his sigh reach across the table and tickle my skin.

Mamma mia. The hairs on my arms stood straight up at attention.

"I was able to book a new venue and tag a catering service at the last minute, but they only do appetizers and hors d'oeuvres." His shoulders hunched a little as he leaned farther into me. Without even a thought, I did the same, inching closer to him.

"This is where I'm hoping you can help me," he said.

"I'm listening." *Listening? Gesu.* Every fiber of my being was zeroed in on this gorgeous guy.

"I know it's last minute and you're probably scheduled to the rafters with holiday orders, but I need a cake."

"That's what we do here."

"No. I don't mean an ordinary cake. One of my staff members was at a wedding last month and said this bakery"—he patted the table with the flat of his hand—"made the cake. He said it was the most amazing thing he'd ever tasted, aside from looking nothing like a cake."

"What was the name of the wedding party?"

"Um, I think he said, Maiden or Madden—"

"Mason?"

"Yeah, that was it. You remember the cake?"

Of course I did, since I'd been the one to bake, decorate, and then deliver it. A six-tiered vanilla pound cake with alternating layers of salted caramel cream and vanilla filling, topped with a white chocolate *ganache*, crumbles of hardened caramel, and decorated with cascading red and pink roses from the top tier down.

It had been a new flavor profile for me, and the bride, groom, and their parents had been over the moon about the taste.

"So, what are you looking for?" I asked. "The same flavors?"

"If possible, but really, I need a statement cake. Custom."

"Custom like…" I waved my hand in the air.

"Something big, like that wedding cake. With lots of, what are they called, tiers? Maybe something creative? Structural, you know?"

Unfortunately, I did. He wanted something that usually takes me days to bake, construct and then decorate. Thanksgiving was in two days, Christmas in four weeks, and I already had upward of fifty big holiday cake orders for businesses I needed to start on. Add in the orders for wedding, anniversary, and specialized birthday cakes and that number doubled. All that, plus the usual daily goods the bakery was famous for.

"And the date you need this by?"

He long neck bobbed as he swallowed. That he was nervous telling me was a bit more than unsettling.

"December fifteenth."

Just three weeks away. Less. Nineteen days because Thanksgiving was late this year.

There was no way I could add another custom-designed cake to my already huge list. Especially at the last minute during my busiest time of the year.

No. Way.

I wonder if he realized what I was about to tell him, because he reached into his coat and pulled out a folded piece of paper. "This is the logo for the charity." He handed me the paper.

Merda.

"The cake is for Pearl's Place?"

He nodded.

"The place that offers free hospice care to kids with cancer, including room and board for the family during treatment?"

"You've heard of it? You know it?"

It was on the tip of my tongue to say "intimately," but for once in my life I did what my *nonna* Angelina instructed me to do more times than I could remember when I was growing up: *chiudi la bocca.* Close your mouth.

"So, you've heard of it?" he repeated.

I nodded. "You support it?"

His gorgeous, storm colored eyes softened. "Not solely. I own a web and app-design company, but I do what I can. The Christmas fundraiser I throw every year brings in a huge chunk of change for the place, so you can see why I'm a little frantic to make sure it goes off as scheduled and promised. I'd hate for them to lose out on such a substantial donation, especially at the holidays."

I bit down on my bottom lip, my gaze dropping to my order book. Being busy wasn't the only reason I should tell him I couldn't help. There were too many memories, sad, heart-wrenching memories, associated with Pearl's Place. I didn't want to go there—go back to those memories, and I knew I would if I agreed to make him a cake.

He sensed my hesitation and leaned even closer. "Look. I know this is just about the worst request you can get from a customer this close to Christmas, but I'm willing to pay whatever you ask."

"It's not the money," I said, although the phrase *whatever you ask* had my mercenary business owner's heart pounding. I am, after all, my father's daughter. "It's more that I'm already jampacked with holiday projects as it is. Adding on another big custom order is going to be tough."

"I think I just heard you say it'll be tough…but doable? Did I hallucinate that?"

Sitting across from me, his face was pulled into such an expectant expression of hope I wanted to laugh. He looked just like my cousin Chloe's son, Lorenzo, whenever he visits the bakery and gets a gander at the filled cookie trays. His eyes go as wide as his *nonna's* fine china plates.

I really shouldn't add another thing to my to-do list.

But…

"Well…" I sighed. "What did you have in mind?"

I tried to tell myself it wasn't because of that adorable expression on his handsome face that I'd acquiesced. It was a wonder the Virgin Mary herself didn't suddenly appear before me and box my ears for lying so blatantly.

"Since it's Christmas, I was hoping for something…*Christmasy*." He waved his hand in little circles in the air.

Since my heritage is Italian, that kind of gesture is like a second language to me.

The tops of his ears turned the same color as my mother's tomatoes when she blanches them. "I'm sorry," he said, glancing down at his coffee mug. "Like I said, my assistant usually handles stuff like this. She's the creative one. I'm more the business end, you know?"

I nodded.

"My company is donating hundreds of tech toys to Pearl's Place this year to give the kids something to play with while they're receiving treatment, in addition to the money we're going to bring in from the fundraiser, so maybe something along those lines?"

Ideas, my father has commented on many times during my life, are his and my shared bread and butter.

"So, how about this?" I pulled my order book to a blank page and started sketching. "Since your event is gonna benefit a place that caters to sick kids, why not something like Santa's Toy Land?"

I draw fast, which is always a benefit when I'm crunched for time. As I hunched over the pad, Connor leaned in, his head cocked, to watch me. He was so close the aroma of something woodsy and clean that he'd probably showered with wafted over me. Now, when you're used to the heavenly scents of dough rising and baking, cinnamon and sugar melting together, and buttercream and chocolate filling your senses twenty-four/seven, the aroma of something different and….stimulating, is enough to make you sit up and listen. Well, *smell*, I guess is the better word.

"How about little techy elves?" I asked, trying not to make it obvious that I was inhaling him while sketching an elf with an e-reader in its hands. "They can be wrapping tablets and hand-held e-games in the workshop."

"I love it," he said, that cute grin pulling across the width of his face again.

My gaze flicked to his hands, still resting on either side of his coffee mug. I'd put his age at high thirties, and by the looks of his hands I was correct. Smooth and without the weathered, freckled, and age-spotted skin of my father, uncles, and older brothers, this man's hands looked like they spent their days at a desk and not outdoors or involved in manual labor.

His fingers were long and lean, as if he played an

instrument, and for a split second I wondered what they'd feel like playing me.

Madre di Dio. What a thought to have in the middle of the day in a bakery. Or anywhere, for that matter.

Look, it had been a long, long time since a guy's hands had been on me in anything resembling a carnal way. My ex had decamped to parts unknown five years ago after signing the divorce papers, and I'd been so busy rebuilding my life that adding any kind of relationship to it wasn't even a notion. Besides, with my hovering parents, one of whom worked for me while the other popped in daily to check up on their only daughter, I had enough on my plate fending off the men they wanted to introduce me to. Guys who, for the most part, had unorthodox lifestyles, carried concealed, and owed my father innumerable *favors.*

Anyway. Just as I was wondering what his hands would feel like drifting all over me, my name was called—okay, bellowed is the better word—from behind us. I looked up to see my oldest brother's son Jerome, whom everyone calls Pesce, crossing the store, a look of concern on his face. At least, I thought it was concern. It was hard to tell with Pesce. At twenty and still living at home with an overindulgent, overprotective mother and a father who considered yelling a form of endearment, this kid wore a perpetual scowl on his chubby, jowly face. He'd stopped growing upward and started growing outward at fifteen, so that now he was almost as wide as his five-eight height. Add in the fact that his nickname was Pesce because he wouldn't eat fish—a mortal sin in my family—and well, the kid deserved to frown.

"Excuse me," I said, rising. My nephew isn't the most pleasant person on my staff and whatever had made him seek me out must have been problematic because he usually stayed down in the bake room, liking the solitude of just him and the industrial ovens.

"*Zia* Regina, you gotta come. Now. The friggin' ovens are whackin' out. Stupid pieces of shit ain't gettin' up to temp."

Did I also mention that Pesce's a lot like his father in the yelling department?

"Lower your voice and watch your language," I said, channeling my cousin Chloe when she disciplines her kids. She, too, was raised in a family where everyone spoke loudly to be heard over everyone else. Meal times sounded an awful lot like feeding time at the zoo when we were growing up. Still do to this day. Chloe learned early on the benefits of adopting inside voices with her children. "This is a place of business," I added. "My customers don't need to hear you cursing."

Pesce had the grace to look embarrassed as he lowered his chins to his barrel chest and snuck a few furtive glances at the waiting throng of people.

"Sorry."

"So what's wrong with the ovens?"

In a much lower tone, he said, "Heat isn't coming up to temp for baking. I think the frigg—uh—the thermostat is on the fritz. We got a backlog now of things that gotta get baked. Whatta you want me to do?"

"I'll be right down to take a look," I told him. "Let me finish up with this order."

"You want me to shut everything down?"

"No. That's the last thing I'll do if I can't figure

out what's wrong. Just give me a minute."

He nodded and shot a glance over my shoulder to my customer. I think his scowl deepened, but as I said, sometimes it's hard to tell.

"I apologize," I said when I got back to the table. "Baking emergency."

He stood. "I won't take up any more of your time because I can see how busy you are. Just knowing that you'll be able to help me has made this day so much better."

He reached into his jacket and pulled out a business card. "May I?" he asked, pointing to my pen. When I handed it to him, a spark ignited between us again. We both jumped a bit. His grin pulled wider, and for the first time, I noticed the little accordion fan of lines spreading from the corners of his eyes to his temples.

"This has my email address on it, but I'm giving you my personal cell number, as well. When you have the order set, just send me the bill and the particulars." He handed the pen and the card to me, then took one of my hands in his. "I don't care about the cost. I really don't. You're doing me such a humongous favor by agreeing to this, any price wouldn't be enough."

It was good thing my father wasn't standing around us. Otherwise, that phrase *doing me a humongous favor* would have taken on a whole new meaning.

"Your idea of a techy Santa's workshop is perfect."

"I'll fax you a sketch when I have it finalized."

"I can't wait to see how it comes out."

We stood there, staring at one another, for a few beats. The bakery was exploding with voices, customers talking to one another or on cell phones, my workers shouting out order numbers, the ring of the cash register going nonstop. But the two of us could have been in a silent tomb for all of that. At least, I felt that way. The noise level was relegated to a low hum, the crush of people almost invisible to me. All I could see was his face—those eyes the color of migrant, drifting clouds, those full lips that had my own tingling to touch.

A subtle squeeze of the hand he held and he took a step closer, keeping our hands joined.

"Regina." His low voice drifted across the hubbub and hit me square between the eyes like a bullet shot from a close range .22. I could hear my pulse pounding and whooshing in my temples, feel my lungs expanding for air. My feet turned to lead. If someone had come behind and pushed into me, I wouldn't have moved an inch.

What he'd been about to say was forever squelched by my mother's thunderous roar. "*Regina.* Pesce's screaming for ya down at the ovens. *Andare avanti.* Get going."

There have been times in my life I truly wished I'd been a foundling. Like during my first choir recital at St. Rita's of the Armada Parish when I was ten. My father stood center aisle in the church hall, filming the entire program with a video camera the size of Montana he'd gotten "from a guy who knew a guy who gave him a great deal." The motor whirred loudly while it filmed, every few seconds making a noise like an old attic door creaking on hinges that hadn't moved in decades.

My face heated to the temperature my temperamental ovens should have been baking at. Whereas a moment prior I'd been rooted to the bakery floor, lost in the glimmer of…something…in this man's eyes, my feet now moved like they'd sprouted Mercury's wings.

I dropped Connor's hand, turned, and then over my shoulder said, "You'll be hearing from me," before sprinting away.

"Happy Thanksgiving," he called above the cacophony in the shop.

Hours later after dealing with the oven debacle, which wasn't really a debacle, more of an inconvenience, and working on two big wedding-cake orders I had for the weekend following Thanksgiving, I finally settled back in my office chair, the monthly receipts review a distant memory.

My order book was on top of my desk, opened to the sketch I'd done and Connor's information that I'd jotted down. His business card was still in my apron pocket. I pulled it out and ran my finger over the embossed lettering.

Connor Gilhooly, CG Systems with a Battery Park location and an email address. I flipped the card over to find his scrawled cell phone number. The exchange was a local one. Did that mean he lived in the city as well as worked in it, like me?

I leaned back in my ergonomic chair, a gift from my four sisters-in-law when I'd opened the bakery, and called Connor's face to the front of my mind.

I'd never seen eyes the color of his before. My cousin Chloe and her husband Matt each have one blue eye and one green one. The rest of my relatives range from the northern Italian blue-eyed, fair-haired DNA, to the Sicilian cocoa-colored eyes and midnight hair that I possess, along with my parents and siblings. But Connor's eyes were a collaged combination of gray, blue, and pewter all meshed together. And they were as captivating to look into as the rest of his face.

My fingertips danced over the card again remembering the sting from the spark that shot between us. What had he been about to say when my mother interrupted him? Nothing romantic, of course. I'd met him all of five minutes ago. Just because I'd found him swoon-worthy didn't mean I'd had the same effect on him. I knew for a fact I didn't. I'm just not the kind of girl guys trip over themselves for.

When I was a teenager, I used to think the reason I sat dateless on most Friday and Saturday nights when all my friends were out with hot guys was because I was physically repugnant. When I looked in the mirror I couldn't figure out back then what was so off putting about me. I was curvy, sure, but my brothers assured me guys liked curves on a woman. I wore my waist-length hair parted in the middle and straight down my back after spending hours working on it with a flattening iron. My face was a solid testament to my ancestry with jet black eyebrows arched above coal-colored eyes. My cheekbones, though, were high, and my mouth, my cousin Gia assured me, was sultry and sexy.

It wasn't until I was a senior in high school that I came to realize the reason boys weren't knocking each other over on their way to dating me was due to my father's ridiculous reputation. No one wanted to be the guy who dated Sonny San Valentino's only daughter. The odds of something happening to the guy should he cause me any emotional harm were thought to be great, and most boys my age valued their lives and potential futures.

And I know how dramatic that sounds. My father, despite what people believe, is not a violent man or a criminal in any sense of the word. Sure, he knows some wiseguys with reputations, most of whom he'd grown up with, and does business with a few who have been up the river once or twice…or more, for various and sundry charges, but he's not the gangster he's believed to be.

Reputations, though, are like rumors. They spread fast and furious despite any semblance of fact.

One nugget of truth to the entire situation that I did discover though, was that my father had been known to talk at the Marconi club where he was a frequent mahjong player, that no boy was good enough to date his little *bellissima figlia,* the name he always called me by. He didn't want me dating and when the time came for me to marry, he would pick out the husband for me. My brother GianCarlo heard this from a friend of his and he repeated it to his wife Trixie, who then told it to me like any good Italian *cognata* would.

Needless to say when I found out, Pop's little *bellissima figlia* erupted like Mount Vesuvius. I went out and grabbed the first guy I saw, got pregnant within a month, and married a few weeks later by the priest who'd baptized, communed, and confirmed me.

And, obeying my mother's wishes, wore a virginal white gown that had belonged to her mother.

The one and only timed I've ever rebelled in my life, and the ramifications of that single action still haunt me to this day.

My eyes started to get heavy, so I decided to call it a night. I had to be up in a few hours to start decorating the cakes due for pickup before the holiday hit.

As I snuggled under the quilt my *nonna* made for my tenth birthday, eyes the color of darkening clouds followed me into sleep.

Chapter 2

Regina's tips for surviving in a big Italian family:
2. Count your blessings and pass the macaroni.

"You look tired, *bellissima figlia*."

"Thanks, Pop. Just what every girl wants to hear when she walks through the door." I shook my head and kissed both his cheeks, handing him four of my bakery boxes with the pies I'd baked, then shrugged out of my coat.

Thanksgiving morning had dawned cold with a bitter wind slicing through the air. The bakery was officially closed today, so I'd been able to sleep in until six a.m., which, believe me, was a godsend because I was—as my undiplomatic father had just stated—dog tired.

"Sonny, why you gotta say things like that to Regina?" my mother asked from her perpetual spot at the stove. She'd gotten her hair done-up, as she calls it, the day before, and the halo of champagne-tinted curls was wilting a bit as she stirred the boiling pot of pasta. "My Regina looks as beautiful as she always does." She flicked her gaze to me and gave me a once-over rake every Italian mother has known how to do since the dawn of time. "Even tired."

Left-handed compliment, thy name is Ursula Rigetti San Valentino.

"Thanks, Ma." I bent to kiss her cheeks as well. "It smells great in here."

"It always smells great in here," my oldest brother GianCarlo (Pesce's dad) said, coming up behind me. He wrapped his hands around my waist and hugged me like he was attempting a Heimlich maneuver. "Did you bring me my pie, *sorellina mia*?"

"What kind of a little sister and baker would I be if I hadn't?" I spun around and kissed his cheeks, too.

That's my family: a bunch of cheek kissers, men and women alike. No one was exempt from the two-smooch *bacio*.

"Yours is the one with the blue string," I told him. "It came out of the oven about an hour ago."

"I'm putting it out in my car so I can take it home an' eat it later when I'm watchin' the game."

My father's open palm swatted the top of his oldest son's head as he walked by. "Hey! What's with the head smack, Pop?" 'Carlo gripped the top of his head, shielding it—I knew from experience—from another hit.

"Since when are you so greedy? Your mama and me taught you all to share, no?"

"Reggie made me a special pie," my brother whined, rubbing his head now. "I called and asked her to make one just for me to bring home. There's still three left for everyone else. I'm not being greedy."

A scowl, the twin to his son's, branched across his full face.

"He did, Pop," I said.

Experience has also taught me that no apology for the head smack would be coming anytime soon from my father. The zombie apocalypse would occur before

Salvatore San Valentino ever expressed regret at something he'd done.

"What can I do to help?" I asked my mother. "Set the table? Open the wine."

"I set the table last night when I got home from Mass. And your sisters-in-law opened the vino when they got here." Ma's lips puckered into a self-righteous line that had me experiencing flashbacks to my grade-school nuns. The presence of it across an aging and withered bride of Christ's face denoted someone in the class was about to experience a little Hell on Earth. Luckily, I'd been spared from the experience. My brothers had not.

"It's a holiday, Teddy. Let the girls have a couple-a belts while they watch the Macy's parade." My father still referred to his wife by the nickname he'd gifted her with more than fifty years ago. The root meaning for Ursula is *bear.* From the moment Pop was introduced to her at a church dance by the parish priest when they were both fifteen, he'd called her his Teddy Bear because she was so tiny and—in his words—cuddly.

I know. My little romantic heart always sighs when I think about that story.

The line across her face deepened. My mother is as old-school Italian mama as they make 'em when it concerns her children. No girls my brothers brought home had ever been good enough for her *bambini ragazzi*—baby boys. I doubt the Virgin Mary would have been good enough in her eyes.

And let's not forget about my loser ex. To this day if his name—or God forbid a reference to him—is made or said, she crosses herself and then spits on the first two fingers of her blessing hand to ward off potential evil from the mention.

"They should be in here, helping me, like good wives, instead of in there cackling and gossiping like old hens. And drinking. *Non è giusto*. It's not right."

I'd heard this lament more times than I could remember over the years. Ma would complain about her daughters-in-law not helping, but the reason they didn't was because they couldn't do anything right in Ursula's eyes. Whatever they did, whether it was set the table, roll out the dough for the pasta, or even open a jar of my aunt Frankie's famous tomato sauce, Ma complained they were doing it wrong. After a few years of this constant haranguing, my brother's wives had all defected from the kitchen to the den whenever she was cooking.

Pop shot me a look, rolled his eyes, and shook his head. He knew the reason his daughters-in-law had decamped. Fifty years of marriage to the same woman had taught him when to hold his tongue though, especially if he didn't want to be on the receiving end of her wicked one.

"Let me help, Ma," I offered again. Because I was her own flesh and blood, the only girl, and the youngest of all her *bambini*, I knew I could do no wrong in her eyes.

Spoiled, much? A bit, yeah.

A half hour later the turkey was carved, the homemade pasta was perfectly *al dente,* and the rest of the side dishes were all set on the table. This was an Italian household to its core, so the usual Thanksgiving fixings—sweet potatoes, green beans, cranberry sauce, and Parker House rolls—were absent, substituted by *tagliatelle*, red sauce—what we refer to as *gravy*—

c*iabatta* bread, and roasted peppers, along with stuffed tomatoes and a huge salad.

We did succumb to one American tradition, though, and have turkey with the meal. The fact that each and every one of us smothered it in Aunt Frankie's tomato gravy, well, that's the Italian in us.

"Sonny, you say the Grace," Ma instructed as we all held hands.

My father stood at the head of the table, my mother seated next to him. As was also tradition, my father never sat down to eat in his shirt. A bright white wife-beater I knew he got by the gross at a discount dollar store a friend of his owned was his usual table garb. And by *got by the gross*, I mean it in the literal way. Pop had crates of the shirts stacked in the garage. It didn't matter that the rest of us were dressed appropriately. Ever since my memory could be counted on, my father sat at a family table sans his outer shirt. Of course if we were at a restaurant or a fancy function like a wedding, he submitted and left it on for decency's sake. But with family, all thoughts of decency flew out the storm windows. Since packing on a few extra belly pounds over the past couple years, he'd started wearing suspenders to keep his pants up because he hated the confining feeling of a belt.

"Hold hands and bow ya heads," Pop instructed. We all complied. Pop looked up at the dining room ceiling. As a kid I'd always wondered if he could see God somewhere floating around the crystal chandelier. "Lord," he said, focusing on the ceiling stucco, "we want to thank you for this food, made by the wife and paid for by my hard work. We want to thank you for our health, the roofs over our heads, the fact we got no bills, ain't no one doing time right now, and most of all for the love we share as a family. Bless this food, Lord. Amen."

A chorus of *Amens* went around the table. Pop sat, tucked his napkin in his undershirt collar, his suspenders draped over his hairy, beefy arms.

"Petey," he said to my youngest brother, "pass the macaroni."

And so we ate.

And ate.

My mother believed in the old adage that if you ever ran out of food at a meal it meant you'd been miserly in the making of it.

Conversation was loud across and along the table with my brothers, their wives, and some of their kids all talking at cross purposes and over one another, each trying to be heard.

Like I usually did, unless someone was speaking directly to me, I tended to tune them all out.

The twenty-five pound turkey Pop had carved was picked clean to the bones. I knew Ma would make soup stock from it tonight after everyone had gone home. At the conclusion of the main meal, my brothers all sat back in their seats and slid their belts open a few notches. 'Carlo had gone so far as to undo the top button on his pants.

"As always, Ma," my brother Petey said, with a drowsy tryptophan-induced grin on his face, "nobody cooks like you. Simply the best."

His wife, Penny, shot him a deadly glare. It wasn't *malocchio*-worthy like my *nonna's* had been when she was alive, but it was close.

"You doin' okay?" my sister-in-law Trixie,

GianCarlo's wife, asked me. She was seated next to me, my mother on the other side of me in the runner's chair, so called because of its close location to the kitchen. Whenever something was needed, the person in the runner's chair was elected to go get it. It really, in all seriousness, should just have been called "Ma's chair" because she was the only one who'd ever sat in it in the thirty-two years of my memory.

"I'm okay," I told Trixie. With a shrug I added, "Busy at the bakery 'cause it's that time of year. But I'm okay."

"You seeing anybody these days? Like, dating?"

Trixie was the oldest of all my brother's wives and the one who routinely asked after my love life. Or lack of it.

"No free time," I said. "The bakery takes up all my hours. When I'm not working, I'm planning, paying bills, ordering supplies. Throw in a few much-needed hours of sleep each night, and months can change before I realize it."

Trixie shook her head, her over-Aqua-netted hair staying perfectly in place while she moved. "You're too young, Reg, to be sitting alone at night in that apartment. You're gonna shrivel and rot before your time. A girl's gotta"—she lowered her voice and moved a little closer to me—"*get some* sometime, you know?" Her raised eyebrows underscored her meaning as her intent glare lit on me. "Don't use it, you're gonna lose it."

"Lose what?" my mother asked in her usual thunderous voice at just the moment the entire table's conversations screamed to a halt.

"Nothin' Ma. Trixie and me were just talking about

the bakery." I hoped against hope she'd let it go, but it wasn't my mother I needed to worry about. It was Trixie.

She leaned forward and cocked her head so she could see my mother across my chest, the few glasses of pre-dinner vino showing their effects. "I was just saying to Reggie that she should be going out, dating. Trying to find a guy worthy of her. Not one like her loser ex."

Remember when I said there were times I'd wished I'd been a foundling? Yeah. This was a prime example of one of those times.

"She's still young and beautiful," Trixie continued. "She's got needs like any young and healthy woman does."

Forget about being a foundling. Maybe it would have been better if I'd never been born.

"Hush with that kinda talk, Beatrice Guilia," my mother said, sharply. She made the sign of the cross over her chest. "We don't talk about things like *needs* and such at the dinner table. There's kids present. *Madonna mia.*"

Once Trixie starts on a subject, though, it's hard to stop her. Not even 'Carlo pulling at her arm can sway her when she wants to make a point. "All I'm sayin' is Reggie shouldn't let the tragedy of her past prevent her from finding lasting happiness. She deserves to be happy. In every way," she added, nodding. "Penny, you get me, right?"

I shot my gaze to my other sister-in-law across the table and sent her a silent, wide-eyed plea to keep her mouth shut.

Penny wasn't tuned into my telepathic appeal,

though. I assumed the vino had something to do with her inability to read my mind and eye signals.

"It's true, Reg. You got no life outside-a work," she said. "You need to get out. Meet people. Find a boyfriend. I know a couple-a single guys at work. I could set you up with one of them."

"Nobody's setting Regina up with nobody." My father's booming voice shot through the dining room. "She wants t' meet a guy, I'll introduce her to one. Last time, she went looking on her own, and we all know what happened."

He looked pointedly at me, and I said a silent prayer for the dining room floor to open up and swallow me. The only guys my father was every going to introduce me to were the ones he associated with. None of whom had modern notions of a wife as a life partner, but more the old-fashioned and archaic ones of thinking of a bride as an unpaid domestic, a carrier of the next generation of sons, and a cook. In essence, a woman who was perpetually pregnant, barefoot in the kitchen, and subservient.

Yeah, I know. This is the twenty-first century, and we live in one of the most progressive cities on the planet. But we're talking about a lifetime of shared social mores and cultural dictates that were infused into my family since birth. Maybe even before they were born.

Change was not gonna happen.

"I'm just saying," Trixie pushed—despite the subtle hand I saw her husband shift under the table to grab her thigh and get her to stop—"she should get out more. She lives in the same place she works, for Pete's sake." She turned her slightly tipsy gaze back to me.

"You don't need to go to bars to pick up guys," she said.

My mother crossed herself again and began muttering in Italian. I wasn't sure, but it sounded like she was saying a prayer for my eternal soul.

"You could go to paint night someplace. Or maybe go bowling."

"Bowling?" 'Carlo said. His thick eyebrows shot up the width of his forehead, almost meeting the receding strip of his hairline. "The only guys she's gonna meet bowling are *pigrones* who can't get dates or guys already hitched." He turned his attention to me and wagged his index finger at me like I was his child and not his baby sister. "Don't go takin' up with any married guys, Reggie. Remember Uncle Joey and that whole Delphina thing he had going on. Almost broke Aunt Frankie's heart."

"Delphina. *Bah.*" My mother made the sign of the cross again and spit on her fingers. "*Puttana.*"

"No good ever comes-a taking up with guys with wives, remember that."

"Good to know," I said, standing with my dish. "Thanks for the advice. Who wants pie? I'll go heat them up."

If I could have sprouted wings, I couldn't have moved any faster out of the dining room. I heard hushed, angry voices follow me as my brothers verbally sparred with their wives.

I took a giant breath, then scraped my plate into the garbage and placed it in the ceramic sink along with the cutlery. My mother still washed all the dishes, pots, and utensils by hand. Pop had tried to gift her with a new dishwasher one Christmas, but she'd waved him off saying she preferred her things hand washed and didn't trust anything mechanical not to chip or crack the imported Italian china she'd been given as a new bride.

I used to wonder if that was truly the reason or if she knew the dishwasher fell off a truck and was worried the police would find out and cart it—and her—off to jail.

I set the oven to a low temp and pulled the pies I'd baked that morning from their boxes. Then, because I knew this after-dinner routine like I knew the back of my hand, I put the coffee pot on, which was already filled with decaf, and plugged in the espresso machine. From the corner of my eye, I spotted my mother waddle into the kitchen, her hands laden with dishes.

"Here, let me, Ma." I took them from her and repeated my motions of moments before.

"*Grazie, mia figlia.*"

"Petey was right," I said. "Everything was delicious as always."

She nodded and began filling the sink with warm water.

"Just a reminder, Reggie. Me, Frankie, and Grace are going to th'outlets in Jersey for some Christmas shopping tomorrow. Get a jump on the sales."

"You know the stores are going to be packed, right? It's Black Friday."

"Why you think we're going? An' why you think they call it that? Black Friday?" She shot her chubby hands to her hips. "Sounds like some kinda plague or somethin'."

Questions like this have pestered my mother her entire life.

Why'd'they call it rubbernecking? We're on a

highway that ain't made of rubber. Why'd'they call it a driveway when we're parked? Why can't they put the fabric softener in the detergent?

I knew this question was asked because that's the way her brain works and didn't necessitate an actual answer. I gave her one, anyway.

"I think's it's because all the stores are hoping to end the day, and begin their holiday receipts, with a profit. You know? In the black?"

"Still a stupid word. Anyways. Your Aunt Frankie's got a boatload of, whatamacallit, coupon books." She waved her hand in the air at me.

"Door busters?" Remember I told you this kind of gesture is like a second language for me?

"Yeah. Another stupid name. Door busters. We ain't bustin' down no doors. If we get there before eight, we get another twenty percent off everything."

"You're gonna have to leave early to beat the traffic." I grabbed a dishtowel and took the now cleaned plate she offered me.

"Grace's coming to pick me up at five thirty."

It was my turn to nod.

"Since you're closed tomorrow, wanna come with us? We could use the extra hands to carry stuff and you're strong."

Again, left-handed compliments were her forte, but I wasn't even tempted. Black Friday and December 26 were the only nonholiday days of the year the bakery was closed. I usually take advantage of the quiet time to catch up on decorating ordered cakes, take store inventory, and even find a little time to soak in a hot tub. If I accompanied Ma and the aunts tomorrow, I wouldn't be able to indulge in that little guilty pleasure.

Besides, I don't know how long I would survive with three women in their late sixties who all talked nonstop, commented—loudly—on what strangers were wearing, buying, or how their kids were misbehaving. Add in that I'd be stuck with them in a car for over two hours both ways in traffic, and, well, having my fingernails pulled off to the quick one by one seemed more appealing.

While I took down the dessert plates and coffee cups, my mother touched my arm.

"Regina."

Her top teeth were sucking on a corner of her bottom lip, and a crater had formed between her brows.

"Ma, what? What's the matter?" I grabbed her hands in mine.

She *tsked* twice, her tongue sounding like sandpaper gliding across jagged, unprocessed wood, and shook her head. "What Trixie said?"

"Yeah?"

"Do you…have you…are you lonely, *bambina*? Do you miss being a wife? A mother?"

We never spoke of this, so I was taken aback by the question. Since I'd petitioned the church to annul my marriage and Pop had pulled in some ecclesiastic favors to expedite the process, my former life wasn't talked of much by my family. I'd made a huge mistake, gone against my parents' wishes and dated a guy so wrong for me on so many levels, then had come to regret it. The ramifications of my actions had started a downward spiral in my life that had ended with death, emotional and physical abandonment, and divorce. Death was as common in an Italian family as making the sign of the cross. Marital abandonment wasn't

33

unheard of, but divorce was the ultimate no-no in such a staunchly Catholic family as mine. It simply wasn't talked about. Ever. For my mother to ask something like this was a shock. But she had real maternal concern in her eyes when she looked up at me.

The need to offer comfort and ease her mind was huge. I pulled her into a hug, my fingertips barely touching as they circled the seven decades of good Italian cooking settled around her waist.

"I'm okay, Ma. Really. I don't miss being married to Johnny one bit."

"But what Trixie said, about you having"—she shuddered—"needs?"

No way was I having this conversation with my sixty-eight year old rosary-toting, church-going mother.

No. Way.

"Don't listen to her, Ma." I pulled back and held her at arm's length. "It's the wine giving her *labbra sciolte*. Loose lips. Ignore what she says."

She palmed my cheek. Her eyes were on the verge of spilling tears, and I couldn't deal with the next question I knew she was going to ask me, so I took the coward's way out, kissed her cheek, and pulled away to get the desserts ready.

"I'm fine. Really. I'm so busy all the time I'm never lonely."

I sent a mental reminder to myself to admit the lie when I went to confession this weekend.

"You work so hard," Ma said. "So you don't have time to think. To remember."

Now my own tears threatened, burning the backs of my eyes. Italian mothers see all, know all, feel all when it concerns their children. Why had I forgotten this?

"The anniversary is soon," she said, in an uncharacteristic soft, low tone.

"You don't have to remind me, Ma. I know what day it is."

"*Bambina*." She wrapped her arms around me from behind and rested her chin on my shoulder.

Ever since taking the commission for Connor's cake, Pearl's Place hadn't been far from my mind. I hadn't told anyone in the bakery about where the cake was going yet knowing I'd get pelted with questions, concerned faces, maybe even a few requests not to do it.

And when your Italian family *requests* something, it's usually not an option to deny the appeal.

I don't know what possessed me to tell my mother, since I was sure what her reaction was going to be, but before I could convince myself not to, I did.

She pulled her arms from around me and then spun me around to face her. "*Regina Maria*. Why?"

A good question. I thought I'd said yes because Connor Gilhooly had looked so worried his planned party was going to be ruined and I'd felt bad for him. Wanting to please people and knowing when to say no have always been at war within me. With a little distance, that reason didn't quite ring true now, and I knew it.

I shrugged. "Maybe, it's time. Time to forget."

"You'll never forget," she said immediately. "*È impossibile.*"

It's impossible.

The oven dinged, telling me the pies were warmed. While I plated them, I told her, "You're right. I won't ever forget. But I need to move on, Ma. You said yourself I work so hard to try and push...everything to the back of my mind. But it's always right here." I tapped my forehead. "Maybe making the cake will help me finally find, I don't know. Closure? I won't ever forget what happened, but I can start to heal. Try to be happy again."

Her mop of champagne curls bounced as she shook her head with the violence of a seizure. "Another *stupido* word. *Closure.* The only thing that ever closes is a coffin."

I winced and shook my head. "Ma."

She beat a fist against her amble breasts in the vicinity of her heart. "Your heart was broken, *bambina*. Shattered. To lose the thing you love the most in the world, the thing you'd lay down your life for, you don't recover from that. Ever. It's always with you."

"I know. It is. But I need to do this, Ma. I need to make this cake. I need to know I can do it. That I've got the strength to."

"Of course you have the strength. You're a San Valentino." Her lips pursed again and her brows tugged forward in that arrogant, haughty way only a true daughter of Italy can pull off to perfection. "You can do anything you tell yourself to."

A moment ago she'd told me I'd never be able to forget the tragedy of my past, and now she was saying I could do anything I wanted if I put my mind to it.

Irony, thy name is Ursula San Valentino.

I'd had enough emotional discourse for the day, so I quickly finished plating the pies, brought them back to the dining room and told everyone I was begging off.

"I need to catch up on a little work, and then I'm gonna get to bed early," I said while I doled out the dessert plates to my siblings.

"You work too hard, Reggie," Petey said right before he shoved almost the entire slice of apple pie I'd given him into his mouth.

"You need an assistant," 'Carlo said. "Someone to take the slack off."

"Thanks, but I'm fine. I like working hard. An assistant would just be in the way."

I caught the quick raised-eyebrows look that passed between my sisters-in-law. Before they could start up with the dating talk and their thoughts about my *needs* again, I beat a hasty *arrivederci*.

I love my family to no end. I'd do anything I could for them, take a bullet, lie down and die for them, help in any way I can.

But sometimes I just needed a break from them.

Twenty minutes later, after taking an Uber back to my place, I shrugged out of my clothes and into my favorite comfort clothes: flannel pajamas.

Seated at my home office desk, I booted up my computer, planning to get a head start on the supply ordering I'd need for the next few weeks. Connor's sketch and the estimated bill I'd drawn up for the cake sat on my desk next to my order pad and a half dozen other bills and orders I needed to upload.

I opened my email, then scanned the picture of Santa's Toy Land I'd finished and attached it to the bill. After writing how the cost might change a little, I then electronically signed it and hit send. It was much easier to contact him via email than to call his cell phone. This was, after all, a business transaction. I didn't call any other clients unless there were problems that needed immediate attention, so I wasn't going to start doing so now.

Not a minute later a response alarm beeped on my screen.

Why are you working on Thanksgiving? Connor's email response said. *I thought you'd be out celebrating the day with your family.*

Already did, I typed back. *My parents eat early so everyone can go their own way afterward without it getting too late.*

So, you're home now?

Yup. Lots of catch-up work needs my attention.

I could use someone with your work ethic in my organization.

I smiled at that. *Don't be too impressed,* I wrote back. *You know what it's like when you own your own business. The buck—literally—stops with you. Speaking of, you answered my email right away. I figured you'd see it when you got back to work.*

I'm in my office now, just like you. My folks like to eat early, too. On my way back home, I figured I'd stop and get some work done. I've got a new app coming online next week, and there are still some kinks that need to be worked through.

I fingered the business card he'd given me. The company address was down near Battery Park, so where had he been coming from?

When you're the boss, the work never ends, I typed.

Ain't it the truth?

It dawned on me that this conversation was the longest one I'd had with a guy in quite some time. Trixie's words drifted back to me. *A girl's gotta get some, sometimes, you know?*

Boy, did I ever.

The lie I'd told my mother about my never being lonely jumped into my head.

I wondered if Connor was…attached. I didn't think he was married because what wife would want him to go into the office on a holiday, but you never know. Some women don't mind that their husbands work all the time. I opened a new window and typed his name into a Google search.

And the second I did I X'd out of it.

Madonna. What was I doing? Connor Gilhooly was a customer, not a potential anything else. I needed to remember that. I had no business trolling the Internet for info on him.

Quickly, I typed, *Speaking of, receipts are calling my name. Enjoy the rest of the holiday.*

I thought that would be it, but I was wrong.

Hey, before you go, he typed, *can I come in some time to taste different flavors for the cake? The guy who works for me? The one who mentioned the wedding he was at? He says I should try different ones to make sure the salted caramel is the option I want. So. Can I come by sometime? Try a few out?*

This wasn't necessarily an unusual request from a customer. For brides and their grooms, I usually put together a few choices and then had them come in to see which flavor profile fit their wedding the best.

Before I could respond, he sent another email. *I can come by tomorrow sometime if you're not busy. I close the business on Black Friday so everyone can get a jump on their holiday shopping.*

I wrote back that I was closed tomorrow too, and then we decided on the best time for him to come around.

I'll see you a little before eleven, then.

Okay, see you then, I wrote back.

I waited a few moments to see if we were done.

I thought we were, but then my email alarm dinged again.

So, did you have a good Thanksgiving? Eat lots of turkey with all the fixings? I bet you baked some stuff. Pies. Cookies. And I bet they were…delicious. I'm getting…hungry…thinking about them.

Madre di Dio. What was this? Flirting, or just casual conversation? I hadn't been in the dating pool for so long I had no yardstick.

I decided it was just polite conversation.

I'm Italian, so the fixings were pasta-based. Haha. But yes, I did bring pies. Apple, pumpkin, and cherry. And a separate mince pie for my brother to have for himself. He's the only one who likes it.

Seriously, how do I wrangle an invite to your house for dinner?

If only.

Did you have a good day with your family?

Yeah, but your food sounds better!

I wouldn't argue with that because it was probably true. My mother is many things—dramatic, opinionated, loyal—but she is also a fabulous cook.

Getting paged, so I've got to sign off, Connor wrote. *See you tomorrow. I can't wait.*

I replied that I'd have some good choices for him and then hit send.

The notion to try that name search blew through my head, and I shoved it back out again. Call me old-fashioned—and with my family, was it any wonder I was?—but it seemed a little creepy to find out information about someone that way. I guess I'm old school, but when I want to know something, I ask, not initiate a cyber search.

And I wanted to know about Connor Gilhooly. A lot. Was he married? Had he ever been? Did he have kids? Was he engaged? Living with someone? Or was he unattached and enjoying the single guy lifestyle? I wanted to know why he looked nothing like his Irish name suggested and everything like a son of Italy.

A million other questions ran through my head as I snuggled down under Nonna's quilt a few hours later.

The one question that kept repeating itself, though, was what did those fabulous lips taste like and would I ever find out?

Chapter 3

Regina's tips for surviving in a big Italian family:
3. Accept you will always be a child in your parents'
eyes.

There's something so soothing and calming about
the whir of an industrial mixer.

I'd actually slept in until six a.m. the morning after
Thanksgiving. Waking refreshed and clearheaded, I was
happy the bakery was closed for the day. A few of my
cake decorators might be in at one point to catch up on,
or get ahead of, the big holiday orders, but they usually
didn't show up until after lunch. I had the entire
morning to myself, a rare and pleasant treat.

Don't get me wrong. I love my workers, and since
many of them are family, that love doubles and even
triples. But it was nice not to have to deal with any
warring or arguing personalities or listen to any gossip.

I washed, dressed in an old pair of sweatpants and
a St. Rita's girl's softball T-shirt, and donned my apron
ready to make some cake magic. For Connor's tasting, I
decided on three flavor profiles that would go well with
the Christmas theme, so I got busy. While the cakes
were baking, I made the frosting and then started
working on decorating a wedding cake for Sunday.

Piping buttercream frosting, adding dragées—tiny,
hard sugar balls painted with edible silver paint—along

the borders of the tiers, and swirling individual flowers and leaves down the sides were mindless activities for me. Truly. I could probably pipe an entire four-tiered cake in my sleep.

I heard someone knocking at the service door and, looking up at the clock on the opposite wall, saw that it was a little after eleven a.m. I'd been working nonstop for over four hours.

"Sorry," I said when I unlocked the door to find Connor standing there, his hair dusted with fat, wet snowflakes, his high cheekbones and the tips of his ears cherry-red from the cold air. "When did it start snowing?" I stepped back so he could enter.

"About a half hour ago. It's really starting to come down, too. I slipped a few times on the sidewalk."

"Give me your jacket."

He shrugged out of it and handed it over. Something spicy mixed with citrus hit my nose and shot a swift sense of longing through my entire system. Connor was busy swiping the snow from his hair, so I lifted the material and took a fast sniff. *Gesu.* If his coat smelled this delicious what would his naked skin be like?

Trixie's comment about *needs* shot to the front of my mind again.

I shook my head to clear it and hung the coat up on a wall peg.

I turned back to him, determined to shove those lust-filled wonderings back down. The thought died on my lips when I got my first real look at him.

The silver in his hair sparkled with moisture, turning it the color of gunmetal. He took a quick swipe through the temples to slick it back and then wiped his wet hands on his jeans. As they had before, my fingertips tingled with need to run them through the thick pelt and clutch on tight.

The day we'd met he hadn't taken his coat off, so I'd only seen him in his outerwear. But through his coat I'd made out wide shoulders and long legs.

Now, he stood before me in a black V-neck pullover covering a white T-shirt, in jeans that some time ago had been blue but were now faded and worn in all the stress points, and his physique was put on perfect display for me to drool over.

And drool I did. I actually slammed my lips back together when they popped open so saliva wouldn't ooze down my chin.

Mamma mia.

With shoulders wide as an open doorway, his torso tapered to a trim waist the pullover barely covered. The bottom edge of the T-shirt peeked out from underneath it like a little surprise. His jeans were slung low, sans belt, and dropped in one straight continuous line all the way down his legs. White lines fanned out from where the pants creased at the top juncture of his muscular thighs, and one knee was a needle and thread away from needing a patch job. Leather loafers that looked broken in and butter soft completed him.

If there ever was a more perfect-looking man, I hadn't seen him.

"Hi," he said, a crooked grin filling his face and sending little sparks of joy down my insides. "It smells amazing in here." His lifted his chin and inhaled. "If the samples you have for me taste as good as the aroma in this place, I may need to move my offices close by."

His grin spread cheek to ruddy cheek, and I swear

on Nonna's rosary beads, I almost came undone and jumped him right there and then.

"Have a seat, and I'll go get the cakes." *Gesu,* was that my voice? It sounded like I'd just run around the Seven Hills of Rome in the heat of August without a break.

I walked into the industrial refrigerator in my workroom and slapped a hand to my forehead. If I could have reached it, I would have ticked the back of my head like Pop does when he's annoyed and wants to smack some sense into us.

Get a grip, Regina. The man's a customer just like any other customer.

Oh, yeah? another part of my brain—the one controlled by my raging *needs*—countered. No other customer makes your heart race, your nipples stand at attention like Mussolini's foot soldiers, or your thighs tremble.

Basta. Enough.

I put the round mini cakes I'd made on a tray, took a deep breath, and then walked back to the workroom.

One look at him seated at my worktable, scrolling through his phone, and the *needs* part of my brain sent a shiver of lust down my spine, landing square in what my mother refers to as "girly bits."

I cleared my throat.

Connor looked up, grinned again, and shoved his phone into his front pocket.

"These are three flavors I thought might work well with the concept for Santa's techy toy land," I said.

"I can't wait." His grin turned wicked, and I lost my footing as little as I walked toward him.

With a slight tremble in my hand, I speared the first

sample with a fork and handed it to him.

"Vanilla sponge cake infused with lemon liqueur and a lemon-based buttercream. This one is usually more a summertime cake, but"—I shrugged—"I think it tastes good any time."

He split off a piece of the cake, held the fork up to his nose, and took a whiff. "Smells amazing."

I watched as he placed the fork on the tip of his tongue, then slid the cake into his mouth. It was next to impossible to keep from moaning out loud when his tongue flicked out over his lips and swiped at the errant frosting across them. I had to swallow—hard—three times just so I could keep the feral sound contained within me.

"This is amazing." He lifted his gaze to mine, the truth of his words in his eyes. "Light and fluffy. Just the right combination of sweet and tart."

I nodded. "That's the point."

Instead of eating the rest of the sample like all my other customers routinely did, he put the dish down and said, "What's next?"

"A ginger spice cake with maple and vanilla cream filling, iced with vanilla-bean-and cinnamon-infused whipped cream."

He repeated the same actions again, splicing off a piece of the round. Right before putting the fork to his mouth his gaze lifted to mine. With a grin my *nonna* would have described as looking like *un diavolo*—a devil—he said, "This smells like breakfast."

I laughed. "That's the maple syrup. I only use the best from Vermont."

He slid the fork home, closed his eyes, and sighed. "I imagine this is what breakfast tastes like in Heaven."

He opened his eyes again and, like before, after one taste, put his fork down. "And last?"

"Devil's food with crème de cacao liqueur, chocolate mousse filling with anisette, and dark chocolate buttercream. It's a huge hit with my chocoholic customers."

"Include me in that list."

This time when I gave him the dish our fingertips connected. I couldn't use the excuse of dry weather today as why a visible spark exploded when we touched. It was wet outside and in, as I kept the workroom humidified to prevent the different kinds of frosting and icing mixtures I used to decorate from drying out and cracking.

No. This little spark was all sexual chemistry and stopped my heart for a moment.

Connor felt it too—how could he not—because he jumped a bit in his chair, his gaze connecting with mine, his brows kissing above his eyes.

Without a word said, he took the plate with one hand and circled his other around my wrist.

I knew he could feel my pulse dancing a wild tarantella against his fingers, just like I could feel his warm breath wash over me as he exhaled deeply. All my senses jumped like when one of my grade school nuns clapped a wooden ruler against the desk to get everyone's attention. The stormy colors in his eyes were almost obliterated by the ink of his pupils as they dilated. His breath hissed in, and his grip, though gentle, was solid and secure as it held me prisoner, and *mio Dio*, I was a willing captive for sure.

This man, about whom I knew nothing but his name, stirred emotions up from deep within me that had been dormant and buried for years. With just one touch, I felt more alive, more connected, more *present*, than I had for longer than I could remember. Maybe even ever.

As his gaze took a lazy, determined stroll from my eyes down to my mouth then back up again, all I could think was this, *this*, is what Trixie meant when she said a girl had *needs*.

I did.

Gesu, did I.

In spades.

Did I move closer to him in that moment, or did he reel me in? I'll never know who moved first, but before I could blink, my free hand slid across his pullover, my fingers luxuriating against the softness of the fabric, and stopped to rest on his shoulder. Warmth spread from my fingers up my arm and through my entire body just from touching him.

With our eyes open, each watching the other, our breaths mingled and joined.

The sweet and spicy aroma of maple and ginger clung to him, but I knew he'd be more delicious than any flavor I could concoct.

Our lips were a heartbeat from pressing together. My toes started to tingle and go numb, and my insides turned the consistency of fresh caramel-infused *panna cotta* as he pulled me closer still. Just when I would finally know if he tasted as good as I'd imagined, the silence around us was split apart.

"*Madre di Dio*. It's comin' down like crazy, *bellissima figlia*."

I jumped back. Connor pulled his hand from my wrist, and we both turned as my father barreled through the workroom door, his coat covered in snow. He stomped his feet while he slammed the door shut with enough force to make my teeth rattle.

"Pop. What are you doing here?" I moved away from Connor and helped my father shed his coat while he removed his hat and shook the snow from it. He stomped a few more times and then lifted his head to look at me. The smile died on his face when he spotted Connor over my shoulder. Thick eyebrows that had never met a tweezer knitted together into a bushy woolyworm as his eyes narrowed at my customer, then turned to me.

"Regina Maria, what's going on? The shop is closed today. I thought you'd be alone."

At thirty-two years old, divorced, the owner of my own successful business and financially sound, you'd think I'd be a brave and confident woman. Most days I am. But when either of my parents look at me with suspicion clouding their eyes and concern grinding through their tones, I become the naïve, overprotected little *bambina* I'd once been and revert to type so fast I'm powerless to prevent it.

"It is. Closed, I mean. I was just doing a private tasting for a custom cake I'm making." I swiped my palms down my apron, my father's intense scrutiny making me sweat like a *puttana* at high Mass.

Pop's eyes flicked backed to Connor, who—*Dio lo benedica,* God bless him—was still sitting in his chair. He put the dish he held down on the worktable, rose, and came toward my father with his hand stuck out in greeting.

"Connor Gilhooly, sir. It's a pleasure to meet you."

"Irish," Pop said.

Connor's smile could have charmed the nastiest and meanest of *vecchie streghe,* but, with a lifetime of friends with prison addresses and who carried guns and knives in their pockets like most people carried loose change, my father wasn't easily swayed by charm.

Connor just continued to smile, said, "American," and kept his hand out.

Pop tossed me a quick glance. With his lips pursed together in a tight clump, he took Connor's offered hand.

The corners of Connor's eyes tightened a bit when my father shook his hand and experience told me why. Pop was giving him his trademark *presa d'acciaio,* the grip of steel. Meant to intimidate and let the person know who was in charge, Pop used it routinely on people he wasn't sure about and wasn't certain he could trust. Half the time the person locked in the *presa d'acciaio* would either wince, or when they pulled their hand from Pop's, shake some life back into it.

I gave Connor bonus points when he did neither. I think Pop did, too, because a tiny grin he usually reserved for my mother and his grandkids, skimmed across his lips.

"I know a guy named Gilhooly," Pop said, folding his hands behind his back as he regarded Connor. "Keegan Gilhooly. Part of the Beantown Bunch. Doing a twelve-to-twenty stretch for a bank job that went to crap."

I could feel all the color in my face drain down to my toes. Before I could admonish my father, Connor shook his head and squinched his brows together. "Sorry, doesn't ring a bell. My family is from Staten Island. I'm pretty sure we don't have any relatives in

Boston."

My father nodded, his gaze continuing to assess Connor's face.

"Pop, why are you here?" I repeated, turning his attention to me and away from casting aspersions on Connor's relations. He usually dropped by daily when the bakery was open, but it was more to check on Ma than to visit with me.

He sighed. "Your mama's in Jersey with the girls, and everyone else is either working, out shopping, or decorating." He shrugged, and it was then I realized the reason for the unexpected visit: he was lonely.

"I knew you'd be here all alone, catching up on work, so I figured I'd stop by, see if you wanted to grab a slice at Mangianno's for lunch."

I slid my hand in the crook of his arm. "Thanks, but I've got a ton of work to do."

"You gotta eat."

"I've gotta get stuff done, too. Christmas is coming."

For a moment he looked so disappointed, all I wanted to do was hug him.

"Look," I said, acquiescing like I always do when it comes to my parents. "Why don't you head on over, order us a few slices and some drinks, and I'll come by when I'm finished with Connor, in say"—I glanced up at the wall clock—"twenty minutes? How's that?"

"*Buono.*" He turned his attention back to Connor. "Staten Island?"

"New Dorp, officially. My folks still live there in the house my dad was raised in. My grandmother lives with them."

"So, family's important to you."

It wasn't a question, and Connor didn't take it as one. "More than anything."

Pop nodded again. "You married?"

"Never been."

Pop's eyes narrowed. "Guy respects family so much, I'd think he'd have a wife and kids. I met mine when we was fifteen. Been together every day since."

"You're lucky. I guess I just haven't found the right lady yet." He gaze flicked to me so quick, I thought I imagined it. When I saw the subtle tug of his lips lifting, I knew I hadn't.

"What are you, forty? Forty-five? Can't wait too much longer or you'll be shooting blanks when it comes to making kids."

The blood that drained to my toes? It shot straight back up again heating my cheeks like I was standing in one of my baking ovens with the thermostat turned to one thousand degrees Fahrenheit.

"I'm thirty-six."

"Huh. You look older."

"It's the hair. Premature."

Pop rocked back on his heels. I needed to stop this line of questioning, but for some wacky reason I didn't. In the two minutes they'd been talking, I'd learned more about this man than I'd known before we'd almost kissed. Connor didn't seem to mind the interrogation. He stood casually, his hands tucked in the back pockets of his jeans, a look of quiet acceptance on his face, as if he'd been grilled before by an overprotective and prying *padre.*

"I had an aunt went gray at twenty. Dyed it bright red to cover it up. Scared the living crap outta me every time we visited her, 'cause it looked like her head was on fire."

Connor's response to that was to simply smile.

"You got a job? Something respectable?"

"*Pop*."

"What?" He raised his hands and tossed me a puzzled glare. "It's a legit question."

"It's also rude. Enough with the third degree." I yanked his wet coat from the peg and shoved it—and him—toward the door, plopping his hat back on his head. "Go to Mangianno's and let me finish up here."

"Okay, okay. *Basta.* I'm going. No need to give me the bum's rush." He righted his hat and slipped into the coat.

"It was nice meeting you, Mr. San Valentino. Have a merry Christmas," Connor said.

Pop waved a hand at him, said, "Irish," as if it were his name, then kissed my cheeks and said, "Twenty minutes. I'll be waiting."

"I'll be there. *Nessun problema.*" No worries.

I shut the door behind him with more force than was necessary. The slam echoed inside the workroom, competing with the sound of my heart hammering.

Mortification doused through me.

"I'm sorry about that," I said, still facing the door.

"About what?"

After sucking in a fortifying, steadying breath, I pushed off the door and turned. Connor was leaning against the worktable, a look of utter calm on his face.

"Being grilled like a steak."

His grin spread the width of his jaw. "Your father is very…" He shrugged.

"Crazy? Ill-mannered? Nosy?"

"I was going to say protective."

"Same meaning." I walked back to the table and lifted the cake he'd yet to sample. "But I'm sorry he asked so many personal questions. If it's any consolation, he does that to everyone, but he tends to get a little more intrusive when it comes to people around me. He tends to forget I'm an adult."

Connor took the dish. "I don't think he forgets that for a minute."

"Are you kidding? Of course he does. He treats me like I'm five years old, not thirty-two."

Gesu, Regina. Whine, much?

"What did he call you when he came in? *Bellissima figlia*? Beautiful daughter, right?"

I nodded, wondering how he knew that.

"I think he knows you're a grown woman, but he still sees you as his little princess. His beautiful little daughter. You're lucky to have a dad like that." He forked a sliver of cake into his mouth and then all the expression left his face. He closed his eyes and tilted his head back. Then he groaned. Loudly. The sound sent a shiver of pure lust down my spine.

He opened his eyes. "Oh sweet Jesus, this is amazing."

I couldn't help smiling. Pride, Nonna Angelina used to tell me, was the surest road to *l'Inferno*. Well, I guess I was heading down to Hell when I died because as a baker, I lived for the expression running across Connor's face right now, knowing something I'd made put it there.

He'd closed his eyes again, dipped his head back a little more, lost in the throes of tasting ecstasy I knew the flavors in my cake aroused. His tongue dragged back and forth across his perfect mouth, making it grow moist.

I did, too.

Grow moist, I mean.

He forked another bite in.

"This is the winner. Hands down," he mumbled around his full mouth.

"Okay. Done." I lifted the two remaining plates. "Want me to wrap these up and you can take them with you? Maybe have a little nosh tonight or over the weekend?"

He stared at me while he finished off the chocolate cake sample. "You wouldn't happen to have another one of these would you?" He lifted his now empty plate. "Not that I don't want those"—he chinned the plates in my hand—"but I think I could go the entire weekend and eat just this cake and nothing else."

A huge, pleased laugh pushed from me. "Sorry, I only baked these three this morning."

Suddenly, Connor stood tall. Holding me prisoner with his gaze, he placed his empty dish down on the table and then reached his hand out to my face.

"I've been wanting to do this since I got here," he said, gently swiping a finger across my cheek. He rubbed back and forth, his touch igniting fires all along my nerve endings. With a plate gripped so tight in each hand it was a wonder they didn't shatter, I stood immobile while his soft, tender touch sent my insides exploding.

"Flour dust," he said, showing me his finger. It was coated with a streak of white.

I swallowed, my gaze never leaving his.

"Occupational hazard," I said. Okay, it was really a choked reply because my mouth had gone as dry as over-baked pie dough.

Connor's lips quirked. He freed my hands of the remaining dishes, put them on the table next to the one he'd held and took a step closer to me, the entire time keeping his gaze centered on mine.

All thoughts of blinking, moving, breathing, fled my brain. Connor came close, so close I could make out the chaos of colors in his eyes. Storm-cloud gray circled around the outer rim, his pupils shaded with a pale morning sky. Like me, he didn't blink. It was as if neither of us wanted to miss a moment of what was about to happen, and I knew something was. Something monumental.

Circling one of my wrists again and sliding his other hand around my waist, Connor gave a tiny tug until our torsos bumped. A hot little puff of air escaped through his parted lips. Crème de cacao and chocolate mixed together in a sweet and sensual scent that had my desert-dry mouth salivating with…need.

My knees started to shake, and I was happy Connor was holding me because if he hadn't, I'd have dropped to the floor.

"Regina." Connor's gaze swept across my face as if seeking permission for what he was about to do.

Silly man.

Like I was gonna say no. Like I *could*.

I gave my consent by arching my back and pressing into him.

I drew in one swift breath while his lips parted ever so slightly right before they touched mine in the barest of kisses that rocked me to my core.

How is it possible for something to be as soft as a butterfly's wings yet firm and hard and powerful at the same time? With no willpower to prevent it, my arms lifted and wrapped around his neck, my fingers scraping across the prickly stubble of hair at his nape.

In all my thirty-two years, I'd been kissed by one other man in a romantic way, and I'd wound up married to him. I had no measuring stick for what a kiss should be like between two people except for Johnny and me.

Connor's kiss was so diametrically opposite my ex's in every way, I felt as if I was truly being kissed for the very first time, that I was a kiss virgin, my lips being deflowered right there in my bakery workroom while I was pressed up against my worktable.

Connor let go of my wrist and cupped my chin, changing the angle of my head. Before I could register why, his tongue slid along the seam of my lips, opening them, requesting permission again.

Permission granted.

Mamma mia, was it ever.

I could taste the remnants of the delicious cake I'd baked on his tongue, but more: I could taste him. His very essence. I swear on Nonna's rosary beads, his very soul.

He was scrumptious. Way better than anything I could concoct in my ovens, that was for sure. It flittered through my mind that if I could bottle the very *flavor* of him and use it in my baking, the world would go mad knocking at my door for a taste.

The front of our bodies met in one clean line from chest to toes. We were so close you couldn't have slipped a sheet of the thinnest phyllo pastry dough between us.

Connor's knee glided between mine, his jeans-clad thigh pressing into my pelvis.

Gesu.

I gasped. I think I moaned, too. I can't be sure because my mind was concentrating on the way he slid his leg back and forth across the front of my sweat pants, tormenting me, and by torment I mean driving me wild with pleasure.

And then I stopped concentrating altogether as he started suckling on my tongue.

Lots of things make me happy. The satisfaction of seeing a customer's face when they take the first bite of anything I've made; my parents when they sneak in a quick kiss when they think no one is looking; my nieces and nephews when they open the presents left from Babbo Natale on Christmas day at Nonna and Nonno's house. But I can tell you truthfully, without the need to go to confession to admit I'd lied—because I hadn't— the way Connor Gilhooly made me feel when he kissed me was by far the best, most pleasurable, most amazing sensation I'd ever felt in my entire thirty-two years.

Bar. None.

He yanked my hair out of its perpetual ponytail and feathered his fingers through my temples to hold my head in place while his tongue continued its wicked, naughty dance with mine, driving me insane.

And this *was* insane. Totally *pazzo*—crazy. Just when that thought invaded and settled in my brain and I admitted I didn't care one bit, something started to vibrate against my thigh.

And it wasn't the giant-sized erection I'd been feeling ever since Connor took me in his arms.

The quivering tickled, and I pulled away, trying to squelch the laugh bubbling up.

"Connor, your phone is buzzing."

His stormy eyes were filled with a heated, drowsy confusion that was so darn erotic, my thighs pressed together in response, clutching around his knee.

"It is?"

We both looked down to where our bodies were molded together. I pulled back a bit, and the sound coming from his left front pocket was more audible.

Connor dragged his gaze back to me. He still had my head cocooned between his hands and as if realizing it for the first time, his eyes went wide and he gave a startled little shake of his head. "Uh…I need to…"

"Get that. Yeah." I pulled back, immediately missing the warmth of his body.

Connor lifted the phone from his pocket and connected. Just as he began speaking, I heard voices drifting from outside and the storeroom door blew open again. Two of my best bakers, Kari and Marianne, flew into the workroom, propelled by the raging wind outside. Both of their puffy coats were covered in snow, the lower part of their faces hidden behind scarves, making them look like fashionable snowmen.

"It's comin' down like a snow-nado," Kari said, unwrapping an eight-foot scarf from around her neck.

"We were blown here from the train station by the wind," Marianne added. "Thank you, Jesus, it was at our backs."

Both of them removed their outerwear, their gazes trained on Connor.

"He came in for a tasting," I explained when Kari raised her eyebrows my way.

"Oh yeah? Of what, exactly?" Marianne wanted to know.

Before I could reply, Connor ended his call. He

glanced at my two bakers who were scrutinizing him like two starving kids in an all-you-can eat dessert buffet line, gave them a nod and a quick smile, then turned his attention to me.

He had that look I sometimes see on my mother's face when someone tells a joke she doesn't quite get: a little puzzled and not sure why she is. His gorgeous eyes lit on me, a tiny line dividing his brows.

"Problem?" I asked.

He nodded. "With the new app. I've got to get to my office. A couple of my techs are coming in to figure out what's wrong, but I need to be there." He took a few steps toward me. Because the two *ragazze ficcanaso*—nosy girls—were still staring and probably memorizing everything they saw so they could gossip about it later, I interrupted whatever he'd been about to say.

"So the chocolate cake is the winner," I said in my professional, bakery owner voice. "I'll make sure it gets made to your specifications. No worries."

With a tiny tilt of his head, he nailed me with a look that was so hot it was a wonder I didn't immolate. His back was to the girls, so I knew they couldn't see him. But they could see me, so I made sure to stuff down the need to jump into his arms again and stuck out my hand to shake his instead.

God bless him, Connor must have sensed the reason I was acting like I hadn't had his tongue down my throat just a few seconds before and was riding his knee like a horse.

He grabbed my hand, shook it once, and squeezed.

"Okay. Sounds good. I'm sorry I have to leave."

"I've got to go, too, remember? I've got a hot date

with Pop."

His smile charmed me straight down to my toes.

My girls watched him shrug back into his coat and slide his gloves on.

"Ladies," he said to them. They hadn't moved from their spots since divesting themselves of their own outerwear. Now, to allow him passage, they stepped aside.

Before opening the door, Connor glanced over his shoulder. "Thanks for the…taste," he said.

And then he was gone.

"*Holy hotness,*" Kari said.

"Who *is* that?" her partner in crime asked. "And is he married?"

I told them simply, "A customer," then said I was leaving for lunch with Pop.

It was good thing it was cold and windy for my two block walk to Mangianno's. I needed the chill to cool my body down from the inferno of desire blazing through it.

Cool it down? Who was I kidding? Tossing a bucket of ice water on me wouldn't have cooled me down.

Chapter 4

Regina's tips for surviving in a big Italian family:
4. Learn to carry your grief quietly in your heart and
lean on your family when you need to.

"Nonno and Nonna are doing good," I said with a sniff. "Getting old, but so are the rest of us. Nonna is a big help in the bakery, but I think I'm gonna have her cut back her hours soon. At this point in her life, she should be home with her feet up on the ottoman watching her soaps and keeping Nonno in check."

I brushed a little dirt from the top of the white marble, then swiped at my eyes again.

"Milania made the honor roll this year. Of all your cousins, she's the one I think will go the furthest when she's grown. Be a doctor, or a lawyer. Although, I hope she chooses medicine. If Nonno thinks she's going into law, I'm afraid he's gonna consider that a gift from God to solve any legal problems that pop up. Oh, Angelina." I sighed and rubbed my eyes. "I look at Milania and the rest of your cousins, and sometimes I get so mad. Even though I love them with all my heart, it's just not fair they're here and you're not. I miss you so much, baby. Every. Single. Day."

The wind was biting as it swirled around me in the empty cemetery. I was surprised I was all alone in my section since it was just two weeks before Christmas.

For the past six years that I'd come on this date—December 10—the cemetery had been crowded with visitors paying respects to their loved ones. Not so today. The weather might have something to do with that. A frigid cold front had snapped in yesterday afternoon and was still around this morning. But I didn't care if there was a blizzard or if the temperature was forty below. I never missed visiting on this date. I never would, no matter what.

In the beginning, I'd come here every day. Sat on the ground and cried for hours. Sobbed until my insides screamed in pain with the effort, and my body wouldn't produce any more tears. Ma had Pop physically lift me up from lying on the freshly dug grave several times during those horrible weeks afterward. Both of them were suffused with grief as much as I was.

Although the passage of time hadn't lessened the grief one spit, I was able to start functioning again like a human being, when I hadn't been able to do much more than sleep and cry before.

Six years. Six long years that seemed to blink by. I know how opposite that sounds, how ironic, but it's the way it feels. The days drag on and on, but the years fly by.

Angelina, my darling, beautiful angel of a daughter, would be thirteen this year if she were alive. She would have already made her First Holy Communion, something she was never given a chance to do, and would be studying to make her Confirmation. She'd be a senior in middle school. A teenager, bringing with her all the hormones, crazy emotions, and angst that defined the age.

I'd started measuring how long she'd been gone

from me in the milestones she'd missed a year after she died. First Communion; first confession. Eighth birthday, then ninth, tenth. Moving from grade school to junior high, or middle school as it's called now. All landmarks in her life she was never going to pass through.

In my mind, I always pictured her as the beautiful, frail six-year-old she'd been when God took her to Heaven and made her a true angel, just like her name.

The hurt never went away; it just eased to the point where I could move through each day without it paralyzing me.

"How long you been here, Regina?" my mother asked from behind me right before she plopped down on the bench where I was seated. She was clothed from head to toes, her eyes the only part of her visible over the top of the scarf covering her lower face and neck. A bright red knit hat, made by my cousin Gia's sister-in-law, sat on her head, her old-fashioned black woolen coat covering her from shoulders to knees. Fur-lined, waterproof boots adorned her feet—feet that didn't touch the ground once she sat on the bench, but dangled like she was atop a ledge. The boots were my Christmas gift from the year before. Bright green leather, rabbit-fur-lined gloves Pop gave her a few years ago were a size too big for her stubby fingers, but like Pop told her at the time, he got them "for a song, so beggars and being choosy don't wash."

"You look...festive," I told her, after kissing the minute amount of skin exposed just under her left eye. "And warm."

"Madonna. Fa freddo, oggi." She shivered after telling me what I already knew. It was cold today. She

repeated her question.

"About an hour."

"You're gonna be frozen to the bone soon, *bambina*."

"No, I'm good. I'm bundled up, Ma, don't worry."

She narrowed her eyes, a gesture I knew meant she was thinking, *I will always worry about my bambini.*

"*Madre di Dio,* it's as cold as a witch's tit," blasted from behind us at the same time I heard crunching, huffing, and puffing come close.

My aunt Francesca, who's married to my pop's brother, and her sister Grace trudged up to the grave, garbed much as my mother was. Where Ma is tiny and round, Frankie is small all over, and Gracie a good six inches taller than both of them and buxom as a pinup model circa 1940. All three of them had the same color of champagne-tinted hair under their hats since they'd all had the same *girl* dye their hair for the past twenty years.

It was Gracie who'd made the loud and, some would say, inappropriate comment, since we were in a holy cemetery, about the witch's mammary glands.

"How long you been sittin' here, Regina?" Aunt Frankie asked.

"Over an hour," Ma answered before I could.

"*Gesu.* You're gonna need some soup or somethin' hot to get the circulation back to your feet," Frankie said, shaking her fur-hatted head.

"I'm fine. Really."

I noticed then that Gracie carried a poinsettia plant in bright red, Frankie its twin with white leaves.

"Aw, thanks, *Zie.* It's sweet of you to bring Angelina holiday plants."

Aunt Frankie pressed her lips together, lifted them into a pouty purse, and gave me an elegant shrug that I knew translated to "Why wouldn't we?"

Growing up, Frankie's daughters, Chloe and Gia, told me their mother and their *nonna* Constanza were experts at what they called Italian sign language. The women in Aunt Frankie's bloodline could make a simple hand gesture or tilt their heads a certain way, and everyone present knew exactly what they were silently saying with their bodies. Chloe referred to her mother as having a black belt in kinesthesia. Luckily, I was able to read that body language well.

"Angelina is our great-niece," Frankie said as she placed the plant next to the edge of the gravestone. "Of course we bring her a gift for Christmas."

Both of them made the sign of the cross once they were done.

"We're going uptown for lunch," Ma told me when we all started walking toward the cemetery exit. "And then getting our nails done at some frou-frou salon Joey gave Frankie a gift certificate to. You wanna come along?"

"Yeah, Reggie," Gracie said. "It's a sad day. You shouldn't be alone today but held in the loving bosom of your family."

It dawned on me in that moment that Gracie made a lot of references to breasts.

"Thanks, but I'm good. I've got a little Christmas shopping I need to do, and I won't have a minute free from the bakery until after the holidays. You guys go and have a great time."

I hugged Frankie, who, despite her tiny size, is as strong as a bull, then Gracie. The overwhelming scent of l'Air du Temps wafted over me when she clutched me to her chest.

With my eyes starting to water from the aroma, I turned to my mother. She pulled me to her and said, "You gotta be strong, bambina."

"I know, Ma. I am." I lowered my voice and whispered in her ear, "It's Gracie's perfume. It's stinging my eyes."

She glanced at her sister-in-law's sister, squinting again as she nodded. "Smells like a *puttana*, I know. But she has a good heart."

"She does. Have a nice afternoon."

She placed a lime-green gloved hand on my cheek, the aroma of the leather negating some of Gracie's perfume.

"I'll be fine. Really. I just want some alone time today. You understand, right?"

With a nod, she patted my cheek and got into the backseat of Gracie's big-ass, new Cadillac, a present she received every year from her husband who got it at a great price from a guy Pop knew in the auto business.

"Can we drop you anywhere?" Frankie asked, after rolling down her window.

"I'm gonna walk to the train," I told her. "I'll be fine."

"Of course you will," she said as she slid the window back up. "You're a San Valentino."

I watched them pull into traffic and said a silent act of contrition for lying to them. I didn't have any shopping to do, I simply wanted to be alone today. It was the one day of the year I took off from the bakery, the one day I needed to be alone with my memories.

I rode the train to midtown and then walked toward

Rockefeller Center to see the tree. When Angelina was five, Johnny and I had brought her here as a Christmas treat, taken her ice-skating for the first time, and then had gone to see the holiday show at Radio City. It was the last time the three of us were together as a normal family. A year later, my marriage was in ruins, my daughter was in Heaven, and I was embedded in a depression so deep, my family feared I'd be lost to them forever.

I bought a cup of hot chocolate from a street vendor, then found an empty spot at the top of the stairway down to the rink and leaned against the barrier, just set on watching the skaters. Skating at Rockefeller Center was something I'd done a lot when I was kid. Growing up in Manhattan, my cousins and I would take the train to midtown after school and on the weekends and troll around Fifth Avenue, staring into shop windows at the gorgeous designer clothes and practicing our love of people watching. We'd gorge on hot chocolate and hot dogs, skate, and then head back home, full, happy, and exhausted.

Tears burned the backs of my eyes while I watched a mom and dad teaching their little guy to skate. Angelina would never have the memories I did as I child, would never know the freedom of living in the greatest city in the world, or the love and devotion of her family.

The boy's gleeful shriek as his dad spun him around warmed my heart and tore at my soul. A laugh choked out of me when he wiped out on his butt, a goofy smile on his face.

To be so young, so innocent, so happy. My daughter would never be any of those things, and it wasn't fair.

It just wasn't fair.

Suddenly, I felt the crowd close in on me, the laughter I'd enjoyed a moment before now sounding like one of my old nuns' fingernails scraping along a bare blackboard. The aroma of fresh chestnuts, a smell that always made my mouth water, was now acrid and nauseating. A swell of bile chugged up within me, threatening. My hands began sweating inside my gloves, so I tore them off and thrust them in my coat pockets. Gasping for air, I tore at my suffocating scarf.

I needed to get out of here, away from the throng of people, away from the chatter and excitement. I needed to run home, up to my apartment, and shut everything out. Shut the door, shut the lights, and shut my eyes and mind against…everything.

With a panicked impatience, I pushed and shoved my way through the crowds lining the plaza and headed back to Fifth Avenue. There was no respite from the hoard of people milling and walking about.

What had I been thinking coming here today, two weeks before Christmas? What did I expect? That it would be calm and quiet? The streets empty and silent?

I wanted to sprint back to the train station but could only go as fast as the walking mob would allow. Ducking and weaving, I cut people off as I tried to escape, murmuring "Excuse me's" and "Sorry's" when I bumped into them. I ignored the angry glares, turned deaf to the annoyed utterings.

I was almost at the street corner, when, out of nowhere, I felt my arm grabbed, yanking me to a stop.

I turned, a scream shoving its way up my throat. The sound died when I saw who held my arm.

"I called your name," Connor said, pulling me with him to get out of the way of the moving multitude. "Didn't you hear me?"

I shook my head, the force freeing the tears I'd tried to keep contained.

"What's wrong?" He pulled me against his chest and wrapped his arms around me to keep me close. "Regina, what's the matter?"

A sob scraped from my throat as I gripped the front of his coat and clung.

"Good Lord, you're shaking like—" He stopped. I felt him lift a hand and whistle. In the next moment, he helped me into the back of a cab, got in, and gave an instruction to the driver. Once done, he put an arm around my shoulders and pulled me to rest next to him. He felt warm and solid and protective, and I melted into all of it. I laid my head down on his shoulder, sobbing still, and closed my eyes.

The noise of the street was muffled inside the cab, and the quiet was a welcome relief. My nerves, which had been standing at attention and firing with an anxious edginess, started to calm, the warmth of the cab and the security of Connor's arm around me dousing my agitation.

"You're okay, Regina. I've got you now." He kissed my temple and squeezed me closer. He reached into his pocket, pulled out a handkerchief, and handed it to me. I pressed it against my face to sop up the tears I'd shed. The fabric was whisper soft and smelled of a fresh meadow. The initials CG were embroidered into a corner.

He slipped his free hand across his lap and gathered mine in his. "Your hands are like ice," he mumbled, while his fingers began stroking my knuckles, infusing me with their heat. His touch was so reassuring, so soothing. Physically spent and emotionally exhausted from the wall of memories and thoughts that had run rampant through me since I woke, I kept my eyes closed and just leaned against him.

When the cab jerked to a stop, my eyes flew open.

After he paid the driver, he got out and helped me from the interior.

"Where are we?" I asked. We were surrounded by the cityscape, but nothing was familiar.

"Come on." He tucked my hand into the crook of his arm, elbowed his way across the foot traffic, and led me through a large wooden door, decorated with a huge holiday wreath and red bow.

The interior was dark and warm, the rich scent of a wood fire burning adding to the pleasant atmosphere. It took a few moments for my eyes to adjust.

"Mr. Gilhooly," a uniformed maître d' who looked as old as my father said, inclining his head. "Your usual table is ready. Allow me to take your coats."

Connor helped me with mine as I glanced around the room and took in the unfamiliar surroundings. The walls were paneled in a dark, burnished oak stain, and every square inch was covered with black and white photographs of celebrities from all walks of the entertainment industry. Connor placed a hand at the small of my back and propelled me through what I realized now was a restaurant. The maître d' preceded us through the main part of the establishment and kept walking us toward the back. The tables were filled with men and women in business suits, the low hum of conversation, soft and gentle. The wait staff meandered from table to table, silently delivering and removing food and drink in a well-timed and rehearsed dance.

"I'll send your server right over," the maître d' told us, after lifting his hand, indicating I should slip into the booth in front of us. Connor slid in next to me from the opposite side so we were seated next to one another in the center.

"Is he in today?" Connor asked.

"In his office. Shall I tell him you're here?" He handed us each a menu.

"Please."

With that he nodded, then left.

I'd watched this entire exchange without saying a word. While he spoke, I took in Connor's appearance. Gone was the casual-guy look he'd worn in my bakery, replaced by what I gathered was his regular business attire. I was grossly underdressed compared to him in my jeans and Henley to his well-fitted suit and tie. He looked like a captain of corporate commerce. Both styles on him, casual and work wear, were mouthwatering. Even through my sorrow, that registered. When we were alone, Connor reached for my hand. "I hope you're hungry because this place makes the best burgers in the entire state of New York."

"Connor." I shook my head, not knowing what to say. He'd basically kidnapped me from a street corner while I was in the middle of a panic attack, whisked me off in his arms to a safe location, and was now going to feed me.

"Are you okay now?" His hand engulfed mine, his natural body heat surrounding me like heated bath water.

"Better. Thank you for…well, just thank you."

He squeezed my hand. "Want to tell me about it?"

Before I could, we were interrupted by our server. Connor ordered water for us to drink and then a separate cup of tea for me. He gave her our orders after asking how I liked my meat cooked.

"My mother always says a cup of tea helps make anything better," he told me. "Now. Talk to me."

I don't, as a rule, share things with people who aren't family. It's just another facet of my upbringing. I'd heard more times than I could remember Pop saying what happens in the family, stays in the family, kinda like that travel slogan. It's clichéd to say old habits are hard to break, but when something is instilled in you at birth and then ingrained in you as you grow up, well, that cliché proves itself true time and time again.

But just looking at Connor's quiet and accepting face made me want to open up.

"Today is a sad anniversary. I lost someone I loved very much."

He squeezed my hand again. "I'm so sorry."

"Thank you. I was doing fine," I said, "until I wasn't. I visited the cemetery this morning, then decided to come see the tree, like I always do on this date."

"Did something happen? Something that scared you, because when I saw you, you looked panic-stricken. Like you were terrified."

"Not terrified, no. There were just too many people all of a sudden. Laughing. Happy. Being together." With a shrug, I added some honesty I never would have to anyone other than family. "I got angry that I wasn't feeling happy."

Connor's eyes grew soft with sympathy. "I think

that's understandable considering what you're going through today."

"Maybe."

Our server brought our water, my tea. For a few moments, I fiddled with making it to my liking. After taking a sip and letting it settle, I told Connor what had set me off.

"I was watching a young mom and dad teach their little boy how to skate. Their family looked so precious, so happy. I was thinking how lucky they were, the mom and dad, to have that. To be a family. Then I got angry I didn't have that anymore."

"You were married?"

I nodded. "Yeah. Young."

"You're still young, so you must have been barely more than a child when you were."

"You're sweet." I sighed and then sipped my tea. "Some days I feel like I've lived a hundred years."

"You're not alone in that." His lips pulled up on one side. He dragged his free hand through that striking silver pelt and mimicked my sigh.

"I was barely eighteen."

"Okay, that *is* young. How long were you married?"

"Almost eight years. I'm thirty-two now."

"Still young. And your husband?"

"He's been gone for five years." I lowered my head, shook it. I hated thinking about Johnny, hated how it had ended between us. When Angelina got sick, he couldn't bear it. Started drinking, I swear he even started using drugs just to ease the pain. He never visited Angelina when she was in the hospital. In the end, I'd grown to hate him as much as he despised her illness.

Tears swelled and then fell again just thinking about those horrible twelve months. The fights. The screaming. The one and only time he'd raised his fist to me in frustration and anger.

"So you were twenty-six when this…happened?"

"Twenty-five when it started. December tenth is the anniversary. Any death is miserable, but one so close to Christmas is, well, it's almost unbearable."

Connor's eyes clouded over for a moment as he nodded. "I agree. Any death is horrible, but when it's someone you love, it's even worse."

"That sounds like experience talking. Have you lost someone you've loved?"

He didn't answer for a moment.

"My younger brother. He died of leukemia."

"Oh, I'm so sorry." I put down my cup and reached for his hands as he'd done for mine. "Cancer just—" I shrugged. "—sucks. There's no other word for it."

"I agree—"

"Here you go." Our server returned with our food, cutting off what Connor was about to say. At the same time a tall, broad-shouldered and barrel-chested, well-dressed man of an age similar to my father's sauntered over to our table. Connor slid out of the booth and was enveloped in behemoth arms and smacked on the back like a prodigal.

"It's been too long, boyo," the giant said. "Too long. You're looking well. Busy?"

"Ridiculously."

"Aye, that's good then. Keep ya off the streets and outta trouble. And who's this vision, now?" He stared down at our table, and I did a quick side glance to figure out who he was referring to. Vision is a word no one would apply to me. Ever.

"Regina San Valentino. She owns her own bakery and makes the most amazing things you will ever taste in your life."

"Is that so? Well, it's nice to meet you, young lady." He reached a hand across the table, and mine completely disappeared in it. "Aiden Gilhooly, this young hooligan's favorite uncle, is me name."

"You're my only uncle," Connor said, shaking his head.

"And happy you should be about it, boyo."

"Like I have a choice?"

It was impossible not to smile at the loving, playful banter between them. Aiden Gilhooly looked and sounded nothing like Connor. If he hadn't told me they were related, I would never have guessed it. Both were tall, yes, but that's where the similarity began and ended. Connor's complexion was olive and swarthy, while his uncle's was vampire pasty, as if he shunned sunlight at all costs. A mop of mostly white hair tinged with faded patches of pale red sat on a head as round as a pumpkin. Eyes so blue they were almost transparent peeked out from under wooly white eyebrows while fat freckles danced across his nose and chubby cheeks.

If I'd thought Connor's heritage was anything other than full-blown Irish before now, meeting this uncle who had Ireland stamped across his features surely would have put an end to that thought.

"This is my place," Aiden said, a cheek-wide smile beaming at me. "And welcome you are, Miss San Valentino."

"Reggie," I said, smiling back at him. "All my

friends call me Reggie."

"And it's delighted I am to be thought one." He brought my hand to his lips and kissed my knuckles.

Charm was stacked into this family's genes by the fistful.

"Now, boyo, sit yourself back down and eat before it gets cold." He motioned for a waiter and held up an index finger. When Connor was seated back next to me, Aiden pulled a chair from a nearby table and sat with us.

"I've been meaning to call," Aiden said, "about that reservation app you set up for the place."

"Trouble?"

"Not at all. In fact, quite the opposite. Revenue's been up twelve percent since it went live. I've been meaning to call to thank ya for forcing me old keister into the twenty-first century."

Connor's gorgeous face split into the most devilish grin, and a shock of pure lust whipped through me making the space at the top of my thighs tingle. How was it possible that just moments before I'd been feeling depressed and miserable, but one look at this man's mirthful face and those feelings dissipated, to be replaced by sensations I hadn't felt in forever?

Madonna. I was glad I was sitting, my nether regions under the table. I was sure they were visibly quivering and shaking.

"It only took me, what?" Connor cocked his head as he laughed at his uncle. "Ten years of asking?"

"Pesterin' and harassing me nonstop, is more the truth."

"Well, I'm glad it worked."

"Aye. Me, too, boyo."

While they'd been talking I'd taken a bite of the juicy burger sitting in front of me and discovered two things. One, I'd finally gotten my appetite back after not being able to eat a thing this morning due to my cycloning emotions, and two, Connor was right. This was the best burger I'd ever tasted. That was saying a lot since Pop had any number of friends who owned restaurants he'd helped finance. And by finance, I mean he was a silent partner. Cash up front with no questions asked, for the right to come in any time he wanted and without the customary call-ahead reservation.

Aiden's burger put every other hamburger I'd ever tasted to shame.

"So, young lady," the man in question said as a tall drink glass appeared before him on the table. "You own your own bakery, do ya?"

"Yes, sir. On the Upper West Side. I've had it for about three years."

"I can tell you were raised with beautiful manners, my girl, but calling me *sir* makes me feel as if I've got one toe dippin' into the hereafter. My friends"—he emphasized the *my*—"call me Aiden. I'd like you to, as well."

"Thank you."

He nodded. "So. Three years? You don't look old enough to vote, much less own your own business."

"Aiden." Connor slanted him a glare.

"Cool your jets, boyo. I meant no disrespect."

"It's okay," I told him. "Your nephew said much the same thing when we met."

The tips of Connor's ears went pink.

"Did he, now? And you still decided to step out with him?" To Connor he added, "She's a keeper, she is."

It took me a moment to understand his meaning. When it sunk in, I felt heat scorch up my cheeks like an out of control wildfire. "Oh, no. It's not…I mean, we're not…Connor's a customer. I'm making a cake for him. For an event. A charity event that he's having next week. He needed a cake and, well"—I shrugged—"I'm a baker. So…" My mouth slammed shut when both men stared at me.

Gesu.

If my father had been sitting with us, he would have smacked the back of my head and said, "What's up with you? You're talking like you're *pazzo.* Crazy in the head."

Connor took a bite of his burger, then chased it with a swig of his water. To his uncle, he explained, "It's a custom cake for the Pearl's Place party."

"Aye, that's coming up soon." Aiden nodded.

"Five days," Connor said.

"Will be you attending?" I asked in a much more lucid, normal tone after taking a deep calming breath.

"Aye." His jolly demeanor slipped a bit, and he looked…sad, all of a sudden. I wondered why. "Aye. That's an evening I never miss. 'Tis a good man you are, boyo," Aiden told his nephew. Something passed between them, something I couldn't read. A deep, shared meaning without the use of words. My family communicated like that all the time. A simple gesture or a one-word response that told a story to no one but the two speaking.

Aiden lifted his glass and saluted Connor before taking a drink.

"I can't wait to sample your cake now," Aiden told

me. "Me boy, here, doesn't give praise where it's not due. If he says your cake's amazing, I can be sure of it."

I tried not to blush, but it was next to impossible.

"Well, now, I'll let the two of you finish your lunch in peace." He rose, glass in hand. "It's busy I am and happy to be so."

Connor stood as well, and the two embraced again. I loved seeing this kind of easy affection between men who shared a family history. Despite my father's habit of nicking his kids on the head when he was annoyed, he was always the first to grab any one of my brothers into a bear hug, kiss them on both cheeks, and tell them he loved them. I loved that being in public did nothing to deter them from showing their affection. It was nice to see that kind of behavior in families other than my own.

"Reggie, darlin', it's been a delight." He bowed, and I had to restrain the urge to jump up and hug him.

"It was nice meeting you, too."

That jolly grin was back as he winked before he left us.

"There it is," Connor said, his gaze running across my face.

"What?"

"Your smile. It's back. Good."

I tilted my head and tucked my chin, but I knew he could still see the blush I was trying to hide. "I think it's impossible not to smile at your uncle. He's darling. My *nonna* would have called him *un uomo affascinante.* A charming man."

Connor snorted. "A charming devil would be more truthful." He reached over and took my hand in his again. My entire body relaxed, infused with a welcome tranquility that had been eluding me lately, today especially.

"Are you feeling better now?" he asked.

"Much." I nodded and, for once, squeezed his hand to underscore the truth. "Thank you. Thank you so much. For rescuing me. For making me eat. For listening. Today's been…harder…than it has in the past. I don't know why." I looked straight into his eyes, and I swear I could have dove into them, they were so inviting, so tempting. "You came along just when I needed help the most, so thank you, again."

"Regina, you don't have to thank me for any of that. I should be thanking you."

"Me? Why? I haven't done anything except collapse in your arms like an ill-timed soufflé."

His grin was quick and deadly. "Cute analogy for baker."

I shrugged because, well, I *was* a baker. As my *nonna* would say*, è la verità.* It's the truth. "Really, though. How have I helped you?"

Something thoughtful skirted by in his eyes as he stared at me. A corner of his lips quirked up, and he tilted his head, mimicking mine.

"In ways you can't begin to realize," he said, cryptically. "The least of which is you're taking on a substantial project for me at the last minute during what has to be the busiest time of the year for you."

I swiped my hand in the air and pressed my lips together. If I'd had a mirror, my guess is my mother's reflection would be looking back at me. "You're paying for that. A lot," I added, stressing the word.

Connor laughed. "But every bite will be worth it," he said. "I've been having dreams about that chocolate flavor combination for days. Ever since tasting it in your workroom."

His gaze shifted, changed, *heated* as it strolled down from my eyes to my mouth. I knew he was remembering the other thing he'd tasted that day— namely, me.

I swear he knew that I knew what he was thinking because his ears pinked again and he cleared his throat. With a subtle shake of his head, he glanced down at his empty plate and then back up at me with that half grin that turned my insides to mush.

"Have you started on the cake?" he asked. "I imagine it's not the kind of thing you can do all in one day."

"You'd be surprised what you can accomplish if a deadline is looming," I answered. "But I plan on starting the baking tomorrow. I should be able to decorate it over the next few days and then deliver it, as ordered and requested, on Saturday night."

"Will you be delivering it, personally?"

I'd thought about it, especially after speaking with my mother on Thanksgiving. I usually do accompany a custom cake when it's delivered, just to ensure everything goes as planned. Don't get me wrong, my delivery staff—made up of two of my nephews—is top notch and professional. We've never lost a cake yet, and by that I mean none have fallen of the delivery truck—literally fallen off, like from an accident—and we've been lucky enough to never deliver a cake to the wrong address, or on the wrong day, or at the wrong time. I'm a little obsessive when it comes to details, so delivery slips are checked numerous times before the cake leaves the bakery.

Sometimes obsession is a good thing.

Connor's event wasn't at Pearl's Place, so I wouldn't be walking back into the space that had such horrible memories for me. A major plus, there.

I told him I would be, and we verified the time of delivery.

Our waiter asked if we wanted any dessert or anything else. I shook my head when Connor's raised eyebrows shot to me.

"Thank you so much again," I said when the waiter left us alone. "You made what was turning into a miserable day so much better." A thought whizzed into my head. "You know, I didn't think about this at the time, but how did you happen to be there, just when I needed—?" I'd almost said, *you*, but switched it to "help," at the last second.

Connor shook his head and said, "Dumb luck. I had a meeting with a new client at 30 Rock. When it was done, I thought I'd take a walk and see the tree up close. I don't get up this way much during the holiday season. I spotted you and called your name a few times. When I realized you hadn't heard me, I sprinted after you just as you were about to cross the street."

My gaze dropped to my hands, folded in my lap as I settled against the seat back. "It was a wonder I wasn't hit by a car. Or decked by someone I pushed out of the way. All I could think about was getting home as fast as possible so I could just shut everything out." I lifted my gaze back up to him. "I'm so grateful you came along when you did."

Watching the colors change in his eyes was mesmerizing. Like the storm clouds they favored right before a rainfall, the expression in Connor's eyes turned dark and tempestuous, exploding with a swirl of emotions I couldn't decipher.

"I don't want your gratitude, Regina," he said as he moved closer to me in the booth.

"Oh?"

Pathetic response, I know, but my mind shut down the moment his hand snaked into my lap, around my wrist, and then up my arm. His grip, like before, was gentle, but I knew if I tried to escape, I wouldn't be able to break the hold he had on me.

"No. Gratitude is the least of what I want from you."

"What…what do you want?"

Why I felt the need to ask when his intent was so obvious I can't explain. Chalk it up to those lonely teenaged days when I thought boys didn't find me worth asking out.

My throat grew tight as he dipped his head while at the same time tugging on my arm. A tiny line grooved between his brows as his gaze ping-ponged between my eyes, searching for…I don't know. Every nerve in my body shot to attention, craving, *begging* for him to kiss me like he had at the bakery.

And he didn't disappoint.

It made no difference we were in a crowded restaurant, surrounded by people eating, talking. We could have been a thousand miles away on a deserted island for all either of us cared.

My toes curled in my boots and a delicious slice of pleasure shot up my spine when Connor's mouth parted right before touching mine. A hot little wisp of his breath danced over me and filled me with his intent. Our lips touched, met, settled against one another.

Connor slid his tongue along my bottom lip, and I opened for him, reveling in the taste of him.

My free hand slid up his jacket, basking in the rich texture of the fabric, to skim across the column of his throat and settle against his cheek. His skin was smooth and clean-shaven, warm and velvety soft against my palm. Connor let go of my arm and slipped his hand down my back. With his fingers pressed against the dip in my spine, he pressed me in even closer. His tongue nipped and sipped at my own as his fingers fanned across my back and kneaded.

Mio Dio.

Who knew the small of your back was such an erogenous zone? He must have first-hand knowledge about a particularly sensitive nerve bundle in that region because my thighs started to tremble and a deep-seated liquid warmth, like warm butter melting over hot morning *ciabatta* rolls, spread throughout my system. A restlessness for *more* shunted through me from top to bottom, making me fidget and writhe for release. I think I moaned. Or maybe that was Connor. I wasn't sure, but one thing I was sure of was that in all the time I'd been married, I'd never felt so turned on by a simple kiss before.

Okay, well, it really wasn't a *simpl*e kiss. More a life-changing event.

The sound of a throat clearing hit me. Connor pulled back first, and it took a moment for my brain to tell my eyes to open and my mouth to close so I wouldn't look like a freshly caught fish with a hook still in its mouth.

When they finally did open, a pink-cheeked Connor was signing the bill the waiter had presented him with. That done, we were left alone again.

Connor folded his hands in front of him on the table. My romantic little heart hoped it was because he couldn't trust himself not to run them all over me.

"I'm sorry about that," he said after a moment, his gaze still on his hands. "I don't make a habit of kissing women in public."

"Good to know."

When he lifted his head and glanced at me, his brows pulling down over his eyes, I smiled at him, hoping to get the same response back.

I did. Connor took my hand and rubbed my knuckles with the pad of his thumb. His grin went crooked while he shook his head.

"I'd like to continue this in private"—*yes, please!*—"but I've got another meeting I need to get to."

"I should be getting home, too. I need to check on the shop, since we've got such a busy two weeks ahead of us."

We both rose and walked to the front where the maître d' gathered our things from the coat check. He gave Connor his and then helped me shrug into mine.

Out on the sidewalk, the day hadn't grown any warmer. I shivered as I slipped my gloves on.

"Let me get you an Uber." Connor pulled his phone from his coat.

"No, I can take the train. It's no problem."

"Already on its way," he said, tucking the phone back into his pocket. "Three minutes."

I didn't bother arguing, especially when Connor yanked me back into his arms. With his hands woven around my waist, we were chest to chest again, a position I was growing very comfortable with.

"I realize I just said I don't do this in public, but…" He kissed me again. "I can't help it."

Don't worry about it, I wanted to scream. *Just keep on doing it.*

I think I might have actually said it out loud, because Connor's massive shoulders started to shake and I could feel the smile pull across the lips attached to mine.

He pulled back and grinned down at me, then laid his forehead against mine. "Regina."

My name had never sounded so beautiful before. Little pops of yearning, like the way dough snaps when it's being fried, flashed down my insides at the sound of my name on his kissable lips.

"Reggie," I said. "I think you can break down and call me Reggie. Like I told your uncle, all my friends call me that. The only people who call me Regina are my parents, and it's usually when I've done something wrong."

A sweet grin split his face. "I have trouble believing you've ever done anything wrong."

"You'd be surprised."

He kissed the tip of my nose and said, "Your car is here."

A black sedan pulled to the curb.

"I'll see you in a few days," I told him before getting in. "Thank you again for…everything."

He leaned into the car and gave me a final kiss, quick and hard.

As we pulled away from the curb I stared out the window at him. Connor stood, hands in his coat pockets, watching me as well.

Peggy Jaeger

Chapter 5

Regina's tips for surviving in a big Italian family: 5. Accept that the men in your family will always think you need saving, whether you do or not.

"I think this is one of the best ones you've ever done, Reggie," Marianne said from behind me. "You should take a picture of it for the book you show customers."

"Already did," I told her. I finished piping the last little row of green holly along the border of an elf's hat and then stood back and viewed the structure.

The cake was massive. Truly. It stood over four feet tall and was six feet wide. A complete Santa's workshop with six cake elves and enough electronic tablets, and handheld game replicas to gift to a schoolroom of kids.

I'd started working on it the moment I got back from my meltdown lunch with Connor. After all the cakes were baked and cooled, I'd begun principle construction with three of my decorators—Marianne and Kari among them because they were the best—and we'd cut, sliced, and stacked, then molded and smoothed each shape with fondant. After a day in the fridge so everything cooled and "glued" together, we'd started the actual piping of the cake pieces. Each elf had taken over six hours to complete, their faces molded

88

from modeling chocolate and fondant to give each of them their own distinct look.

"Whatever this guy is paying you for this cake," Kari said as she finished attaching a row of blown "snow" made from confectioner's sugar to the window of the toyshop, "isn't enough."

"Let's get it into the fridge for an hour. We don't need to leave to deliver it until six," I said. I'd worked down to the zero hour on this concoction, knowing I wanted each detail to be perfect for Connor.

Connor.

He'd been on my mind continuously these past five days. He'd texted me twice in the Uber and asked me to let him know when I was back at the bakery, safe and sound. I'd complied, telling him again how thankful I was that he'd rescued me.

His cryptic response had been to tell me we'd rescued one another.

He'd called me at least once a day to check up on me, usually at night after I was already tucked in bed, my hands stiff and exhausted from decorating the never-ending orders of holiday cakes and cookies all day long. The launch of the new client app, he'd told me, was taking up so much of his free time he never had a moment to call me during the day.

I didn't mind. There was something so personal, so…intimate about talking with him when everyone was gone for the day and probably snuggled into their own beds. Almost as if no one but the two of us were awake in the world. Just hearing his husky, tired voice did something to my insides. While he told me about his day, comically recalling how one of his techs had proposed to another of his employees by printing a life sized series of emojis set up in a puzzle form, or how frustrating a new client was being, demanding changes to a ready-to-launch app, I imagined him sitting across from me at the dinner table. I'd conjure images of him coming through the door to our home, sweeping me into his arms telling me how much he missed me. Then showing me.

I've never been *that girl*. The kind who fantasized about a man, eternal love, and the whole happily-ever-after thing. Not since the reality of my marriage failing and my daughter dying became my actual life. Nowadays, my fantasies circled around making payroll and possibly taking a few days' vacation someday to Venice or Florence when I was secure enough in the knowledge that the bakery wouldn't burn to the ground if I was away from it for more than a day and not managing every single thing that went on in it.

But just hearing Connor share his day with me, thoughts of how it would be to have someone like him in my life, loving me and wanting to spend the rest of his life with me, gave me hope that it could actually happen.

I'd never had a true courtship with my ex, Johnny, or even a meaningful conversation before we'd been forced to get married. He was guy I knew from school but not one I'd ever hung out with, or who knew my brothers or anyone connected to me. Johnny was opposite to my family in every way conceivable, and that's why I'd gone after him like a house on fire. With the wisdom of age and tragedy, I'd come to see what I'd done as the ultimate rebellion against my overprotective parents and their archaic way of thinking about girls.

And just look where that insurgence had landed me. A childless workaholic divorcee who hadn't had a date since she was seventeen and had kissed two guys in her entire life, slept with just one. So when Connor took the time—his free time—to call me after a trying day just to check in and talk, I'll admit it made me feel all kinds of special.

"You gonna go with the boys to deliver it?" Kari asked.

I nodded.

"Bonus," Marianne said. "You get to see tall, dark, and hunky again." She wiggled her eyebrows at me, a suggestive grin tugging at her lips.

While the two of them starting laughing and going back and forth with all their thoughts about Connor, their own boyfriends, and guys in general, I pushed the cake on its tray back into the storage refrigerator and then went out front to see how the display cases were doing with stock. Ten days before Christmas and my regular customers were starting to purchase all their treats for holiday visiting and house parties.

I glanced around the crowded storefront when I came up the stairs. The display cabinets were being restocked, the line was snaked around the bakery's interior and out the door, and the cash registers were making beautiful Christmas music with all the chiming as each sale was rung up. I didn't see my mother in her usual spot behind the counter, so I did a quick eye roll through the place and found her. She was seated at one of the customer tables with my father, a cup of coffee in front of each of them. Pop was holding one of her hands as he was speaking.

After fifty-plus years of marriage, my mother still

stared at my father as if he hung the moon for her. I simply adore this. Who, in this day and age, can boast that their parents still love and honor each other after decades of family strife, deaths, crises, and war, and can gaze at one another as if they were teenagers finding first love?

This is what fantasies are made of.

"Hey, Pop." I kissed the top of his head and pulled out the empty chair at their table. "What are you doing here?"

"I was out making the rounds and I missed your mama, so I figured I'd come in and steal her away for a few minutes."

See? I love this.

"You need me for somethin', Regina Maria?" Ma asked.

"Nope. Just checking on how everything's going on up here before I have to leave for a delivery."

Her lips pressed together into a line, and she lowered her head to stare at me from under her eyelashes. Why I tend to forget she knows everything that goes on inside my shop, despite only working at the counter, never ceases to surprise me. Of course she knew what cake I was delivering today. She'd probably circled the date on her internal calendar as a reminder.

Pop frowned when he noticed the look Ma was throwing my way. Fifty-plus years of staring across the breakfast table at your spouse every day can make you pretty attuned to the other's expressions, and Pop had a black belt in reading Ma's face.

"This the big-ass Pearl's Place order?" he asked me.

And of course Ma had told him about it. Why

would I ever think she wouldn't share that?

"Not specifically there. It's for a fundraiser that will benefit it."

"So you don't gotta actually deliver it to the hospice?"

"No."

"Good. You should never even have to think about that place, much less go there, again. Gave you enough sad memories for a lifetime, *bellissima figlia.*"

He reached over and grabbed my hand, squeezed it twice, and then glanced over at my mother.

"I know, Pop. But it's been six years. I'm—well, not *over* it. But I can handle the sadness now. Much better than I could when Angie…died."

At the word, my mother made the sign of the cross, kissed her palm, and then leaned over to kiss my cheek. Unexpected tears stung. I tried to blink them away before my parents could notice them, but that's the thing about my parents: they're both acutely tuned in to their children, despite the fact all five of us are adults.

"You don't have to deliver it, you know, Regina," Ma said. "Nunzie and Alby are responsible. They can be counted on to do a good job."

"I know, Ma. But I'm okay to do this, I really am. Besides—" I stood and took a quick swipe at my eyes. "—it's my bakery, and I'm the one who worked on the cake for the past five days. I want to see the expression on Con—uh, *everyone's* faces, when I bring the cake in. The girls think it's my best one yet, and I kinda agree."

"Every cake you do is a masterpiece," Pop said, no small amount of pride in his voice. "If youse was around in the olden days, you woulda been one of them old-world masters, only not a master 'cause you're a girl. But you know what I'm saying."

"I do, Pop, and thanks." I kissed his cheek this time, then bent to do the same to my mother. "You two finish your visit. Drink your coffee. I've gotta get ready."

"You're coming for supper after Mass tomorrow, *si?*"

"Yeah, Ma. I'll be there. I'll bring some cookies for dessert."

"Bring a couple-a boxes," Ma ordered. "And nothing special for your brothers this time. Let their wives bake for them if they want pies and stuff. They don't do much of anything else aside from get their nails painted and shop. It'll do them good to do something other than spend money."

Remember I told you that no one was ever going to be good enough for my mother? Proof of that, right here.

I ran up to my apartment and did a quick check in the mirror. When I delivered cakes to events, I usually went directly from the workroom, apron on, my usual jeans and T-shirt under it. I wasn't a guest and was never asked to stay and take part in the festivities. I figured that wouldn't change with this delivery, but since I was going to be seeing Connor, even if it was for a scant few minutes, I didn't want to look like something the family cat had hocked up after a night on the prowl. I ran a comb through my hair, then pulled it back into a much less wild-looking ponytail, swiped some concealer over the purple splotches under my eyes, and brushed my teeth. This was about as much as I ever did in the way of enhancement, and for the first time in maybe forever, it didn't feel like enough.

I've been gifted with my ancestors' coloring, so my eyelashes are naturally black and I don't need mascara to highlight them. My eyebrows could have done with a major rework, but I was always afraid to do it myself. Trixie, Penny, and my two other sisters-in-law, Carlotta and Ella, had volunteered to take me to their stylist, but all four of them had those plucked-to-one-thin-hair eyebrows that made them appear perpetually surprised, and I didn't think that look would work on me. It didn't on them, either, but I kept my opinion on that to myself.

The one concession I did make was to shed my apron and don my professional chef/baker jacket. I'd had it embroidered with the shop's name and an appliqué of a three tiered cake.

Satisfied this was as good as I was going to get, I went back to the workroom and commandeered the moving of the cake tray into my delivery van.

With my two nephews, Nunzio and Albert (Nunzie and Alby) we managed to get the cake secured into the back of the truck, Alby riding shotgun with it, while Nunzio and I sat up front with him at the wheel.

Ten days before Christmas in Manhattan on a Saturday evening is not my favorite time of the day, year, or place to be driving. The one lucky thing I had on my side was the venue Connor had been able to book at the last minute was on the West Side—the same as my bakery—and only one mile south. It took us almost thirty minutes to drive the twenty blocks and one avenue, but I think that was a record in quick-time for us. Nunzie found the deliveries-only sign and parked the van at the back door. I sent Alby into the front to get the manager to let us in and show us where to bring the cake.

"This place is nice," Nunzie said, looking around as we wheeled the cart along the hallway. "Fancy. Think it's pricey?"

I shrugged. "Probably. Why?"

"I wanna take Paula someplace nice for dinner. Classy, like."

Paula was Nunzie's girlfriend. His parents were her parents' best friends. These two had known one another since birth, been buddies on the playground, first crushes in grade school, and had exclusively been a couple since eighth grade. Nunzie had never kissed another girl. I knew this as a fact because he told me at least once a month.

I took a good look at the furnishings in the main dining area as we were led past it to a separate space reserved for the party.

"You may need to do some overtime, or take a second job, just to be able to pay the bill," I told him.

"Paula's worth it," he replied. "I'm thinking we may get engaged soon. She's the first girl I ever kissed (*see?*), and she's gonna be the last."

I wanted to tell him he was too young to make a decision like that. They both were. But I bit my tongue and held the thought. Who was I to give relationship advice? My Uncle Joey, Pop's brother, has this saying he tugs out every now and again when we're talking— okay, gossiping—about people at the dinner table: *Sometimes you gotta let a person make their own mistakes before they realize what's what.*

Profound? I don't know, but I think it rings true.

The manager opened a ceiling-tall set of double doors for us, and we wheeled the tray through them. The room was huge. Gargantuan-huge. Hundreds of poinsettia plants lined the floor around the room, stacked against the walls two deep, and a Christmas fir that had to be twenty feet or more was planted in a corner, decorated from top branch to trunk with bright white lights and the standard plethora of colored-glass-ball ornaments.

Uniformed servers roamed about, finger foods and flutes of what looked like champagne nestled on their trays. From a raised stage taking up one wall, a six-piece band was belting out holiday tunes. About twenty round tables of ten chairs apiece circled the room around a dance floor already filled with people. Above the band was a banner with the logo for Pearl's Place, a stuffed teddy bear with a band-aid covering one of its arms. Just quick glance at it and a cauldron of heated emotions bubbled up inside me. I looked away and found Connor crossing the dance floor, aiming straight for me, a mile-wide smile crossing his face.

He was wearing a tuxedo.

Holy Mary, mother of God.

In casual clothes, he'd been handsome; in a suit, gorgeous. But in a tuxedo that fit his door-wide shoulders to perfection, he was magnificent. Oversized marble statues of Roman gods couldn't hold a candle to this flesh and blood man. Michelangelo's *David* looked like a puny, doughy teenager compared to Connor Gilhooly decked out in what Pop calls *wedding duds.* His hair was slicked straight back from his forehead, those little salt and pepper flecks at his temples vibrant against the silver mane.

The closer he came, the faster my heart pounded, the more my toes tingled, and the quicker my breathing got.

His gaze never left mine the entire time he crossed the room.

"You're right on time," he said when he finally reached us. With an ease as if he did it every day of his life, Connor pulled me to him, wrapped his arms around my waist, and kissed me full on the lips without a moment's hesitation. He tasted of sweet champagne and Heaven. I think I got a little drunk from just that kiss.

Or maybe it was just seeing him in all his hotness that got me tipsy. It's a toss-up.

It dawned on me that he was kissing me in a public place in full view of all the people attending the fundraiser—and my two nephews. From behind me, I heard a noise like a big dog growling. When I pulled away from Connor's kiss and looked over my shoulder, my nephews looked remarkably like their fathers—my brothers—when they were gearing up for a fight. And by a fight, I don't mean a verbal one.

"Boys," I said, "this is Mr. Gilhooly. Our customer."

I hoped—wished—they'd get the hint and realize they didn't have to defend my honor or any other antiquated notion instilled in them by their fathers and grandfather about their aunt Regina.

Connor was unaware of the tension radiating from these two testosterone-fueled twenty-somethings. Or if he was, he hid it well.

"Guys." He nodded to them, never dropping his smile.

"Where do you want us to put the cake?" I asked, diverting his attention back to me.

His gaze darted from the top of the structure, across the front of Santa's workshop, and then stopped to inspect an elf holding an e-tablet. His lips pulled back into a grin filled with childish glee and mirth. When he turned to me, that boyish glee turned to full adult male, hot and so darn sexy I had to stop myself from panting.

"You're amazing," he said. He pulled me back into a hug before I could stop him, the entire front of my body aligned with his. If we hadn't been in a public forum, surrounded by people, including my two gossipy, tattletale nephews, I would have clung to him for the rest of the night and lost myself in all the hard, fabulous feel of him.

The rest of the night? More like the rest of my life.

"The sketch was good," he said, letting me go, "but the actual structure is beyond perfect."

"Connor?"

In unison, we turned to the sound of the voice. A strikingly beautiful woman a few years younger, several inches taller, and much less round than my mother walked toward us, her gaze flitting from Connor, to me, and then back to him. A stunning silver lamé dress fell from shoulders a handspan wide and down a lithe body I could only ever dream about possessing. My thigh was wider than this gorgeous woman's hips. Hair the color of warm buttermilk fell to her shoulders, straight as an edge of paper, and swayed effortlessly across her skin with each step she took.

"Mom, come meet Regina."

Mom?

"Ah, your baker." Eyes the color of cultivated periwinkles zeroed in on me again. A warm, welcoming smile lit her face as she extended her hand. "Connor's told me so much about you and your bakery," she said.

"It's wonderful to meet you."

I slipped my hand into hers, and the first thought that popped into my head was how similar her son's hand was to his mother's. Warm and smooth. Friendly and pleasant.

"It's lovely to meet you, Mrs. Gilhooly. These are two of my nephews." I waved my free hand over to the boys. "Nunzio and Albert. They work for me at the bakery. They're my delivery team."

The same smile she'd given me she extended to them. The boys, never known for being shy, reserved, or quiet, suddenly turned mute.

"Connor's told us that the flavor of this cake will put us off any other cake for the rest of our lives," his mother said. "We'll be so spoiled, we won't want to eat any other kind but yours."

I squinched up my nose and, addressing him, said, "Thanks. No pressure, there," to which mother and son laughed.

"It's the truth," Connor said.

"My son rarely gives praise, so if he says it's the best cake we'll ever taste, I'm sure it's going to be."

"Ah, an' there she is. The vision."

A huge smile broke on my face when Aiden Gilhooly, decked in a tuxedo similar to his nephew's, trotted up to us, a glass in one hand, a plate in the other.

"Take these, boyo, so I can greet the lovely Miss San Valentino properly." He shoved both at Connor. When his hands were free, he pulled me into a full body hug and lifted me off the floor. " 'Tis pleased I am to see you again, Reggie darlin'."

"Aiden, put the girl down," Connor's mother said, laughter ringing in her voice.

He did as commanded, a pout protruding his lips.

"Ah, Molly, me love, you spoil an old man's fun."

"Old man, my ass," Connor mumbled, loud enough to be heard. "Juvenile delinquent is more like it."

"Watch your manners, now, boyo. You're not old enough that a tick on the old noggin' wouldn't be past me."

"My father still does that to my brothers," I said. "The oldest is forty-nine, and I think he gets ticked the most."

"Deserving of it, I'm sure, just like this one," Aiden said, cocking his chin at Connor.

"Usually," I replied.

"*Zia Regina?*"

I turned to Alby. The question in his wide eyes was obvious.

I repeated my question to Connor before we'd been interrupted.

"Over by the band," he said, pointing to a spot across the dance floor. "I want everyone to be able to see it before it's cut into."

I nodded and the boys maneuvered the cart around the dance floor, Connor's mother and uncle leading the way.

I was all set to follow them, but Connor grabbed my arm. "Regina." His voice was thick with emotion, so much so I felt my feet root to the floor. "I'm so glad you're here. I've been watching for you since I arrived," Connor said.

Awww. That was so sweet.

"You'll stay, won't you?" he asked. "I know I didn't ask if you would before, but I'm really hoping you will."

"Oh. I hadn't planned to, Connor. I usually don't. Just deliver the cake and then…skedaddle."

He took a step closer, and I had to tip my head back to maintain eye contact.

"Well, I'm not going to let you skedaddle"—he grinned so deep his eyes almost closed—"tonight. I want you to stay. Please?"

"But I'm not dressed right for this." I waved my hand around the room. "Everyone's decked out for a fancy party." I ran my hand down my uniform coat. "I stick out like a sore thumb."

He pulled me in even closer, so close our bodies bumped. In a low, sensual voice that had all the parts of me that made me a girl screaming on high alert, he said, "I think you look perfect. And beautiful. Did I mention perfect?"

Mamma mia, this guy was too much. And by too much, I mean he was *perfetto*. Perfect.

"Please stay. It'll mean so much to me if you do. So much."

There was no way I could leave now. Not after that.

Nunzie and Alby had positioned the cake and were on their way back over to me.

"Just give me a minute with my nephews."

Connor nodded, squeezed my arm, and then let me go.

"All set," Nunzie told me.

"Great. I'm going to stick around for a while, so you two take the van and head back."

"How you gonna get home?" Alby asked, his thick brows pulling low over his eyes.

"I'll take a cab."

"One of us can come back and get you," Nunzie said, nodding at his cousin. "You shouldn't be taking cabs at night in the city."

"Yeah, it's not safe. Creeps everywhere on the lookout for helpless females."

Dear God, please deliver me from the overprotective men in my family. I was almost twice their age, and they were acting like I was a kid. Or worse, a frail, elderly lady who needed help to cross the street.

"Don't worry. I'm a big girl. I'll be fine. Now go. Go meet up with your girlfriends and enjoy yourselves. It's almost Christmas."

They shot a look at one another, neither happy about leaving me alone. Really, what did they think was going to happen to me in a crowded ballroom while I served cake?

Finally, they each shrugged with fatalistic acceptance and looked so much like their fathers and grandfather, I grinned. They each kissed my cheek telling me to stay safe.

"All good?" Connor asked as he came up to me.

Grinning, I shook my head and fisted my hands on my hips. "They're so much like their fathers it's spooky. But yeah, everything's cool."

"Here." He handed me a champagne flute.

After a sip of the delicious dry bubbly, I licked my lips and almost stopped breathing when I heard Connor hiss in a breath. His eyes were zeroed in on my mouth, his open lips parted as he continued to stare down at me. Just as he began to lower his head to mine, his name was called. His gaze flicked back to my eyes, and there was such a deep well of want staring back at me, I almost dropped my flute.

"The manager asked me something I don't have a clue about," his mother said. "Can you speak to him?"

"Sure. Be right there, Mom." He turned back to me. "Don't leave. Don't even move. Stay right here, okay? I'll be right back. Stay."

"Connor, really. Stop speaking to the girl like she's a dog," his mother chided.

When he winced, I laughed. "You kinda were," I said.

"Just...don't move."

I saluted him.

When we were alone, Connor's mother regarded me through inquiring eyes, with a grin tugging at her lips. "You, young lady, have made quite an impression on my son. And Aiden. I think the man is half in love with you."

Was she speaking of her son or brother-in-law?

I couldn't help the blush that spread up my cheeks, but I could ignore it and hope she did as well. "I think your son is impressed with the flavor profile of the cake. He, like so many people, seems to favor chocolate."

"Oh, Lord, we're a family of chocoholics." She shook her head and grinned at me. "When Connor was little, the surest way to get him to behave was to threaten to take away any chocolate candy he was promised. He always acted like a little angel whenever my husband or I said no to after-dinner treats if he was naughty."

I laughed with her. "Was your other son the same way?"

Her brows drew together, and she cocked her head

at me, a look of confusion dancing across her eyes.

"Excuse me?" she said.

"Your other son. Was he a chocolate lover, too?"

"I'm sorry, but I don't have another son. Connor is my only child."

Now it was my face that must have looked confused. Hadn't Connor told me that he had a younger brother who'd died of leukemia? Had I imagined that? Before I could explain my question, Connor trotted back to us.

"All fixed now. Mom, Dad's looking for you. He wants a dance."

She rolled her eyes. "Of course he does. Whenever he drinks champagne, he thinks he's Fred Astaire. Say a prayer for my feet."

With a smile, he said, "Alone at last," and clicked his flute to mine.

I wanted to tell him what his mother had just said, but I didn't. I don't know why not. Maybe it was because of the way he was smiling down at me, like I was the only girl in the world. I'd never been looked at before with such…intention, and it made me stop in my mental tracks and just bask. Connor relieved me of my glass and placed it and his down on a table before he wrapped his hand around my elbow and propelled me toward the dance floor.

"There's no way I'll ever mistake myself for Fred Astaire," he said with a chuckle, "but dancing sounds pretty good right now. It gives me total permission"—he slid a hand around my waist—"to hold you in my arms again."

Had I said this guy had charm exploding in his DNA? Charm was too calm a word. Pure, unadulterated magnetism would be more the appropriate term.

Settled in his arms, my head resting against his chest, I felt more content than I had in years. The solid, steady beat of Connor's heart against my ear filled me with a sense of comfort and protection. Why? I hadn't a clue. But being held by him, encircled in strong arms that held me as if I were something fragile and cherished, made me feel just that way. Fragile was a word I'd never used to describe myself. Being cherished, though, was something I'd longed for.

I'd met this man less than five times in my life, and yet there was such an intense connection between us, it was as if we'd always been searching for, and had finally found, one another.

Incredible? Yes. Impossible? Probably. But I knew, knew deep down in what my parish priest calls *mia anima*—my soul—that Connor Gilhooly was destined to be an important part of my life.

In the middle of a dance floor, ten days before Christmas, with a man I knew next to nothing about, my heart unlocked itself from its self-imposed prison after being battered and broken by loss and desertion and was set free.

I wasn't scared, which believe me I should have been. No. If I was anything, I was hopeful. Hopeful that once I let my heart open again, it would fill with love, replacing the sadness that had locked it away.

"You've been busy since the last time I saw you," Connor said. The deep reverberations of his voice bounced through his chest.

"Ridiculously so." I lifted my head and slanted him a look. "I had a last-minute order from a very demanding customer who insisted on a custom cake. He wanted it delivered personally and then had the audacity to make me stick around to cut it."

"Well, since you'd probably be the best one to do that, that makes sense, but it's not the reason I asked you to stay."

"Oh?"

The music changed to a livelier Christmas pop song. Connor sighed and took my hand. "Come on."

He pulled me along with him, sliding past the other dancers and off the dance floor, back to the table he'd placed our glasses on.

"Regina?"

We both looked up as a tall, beautiful African American woman wound her way through tables and chairs. "I thought that was you."

A face from the past smiled at me.

"Sharla."

She pulled me into a full body hug, which I returned without thinking. Her arms stretched around me, and just like the last time she'd held me this way, the aroma of fresh picked peaches drifted around me.

"Let me look at you, girl." She held me at arm's length, a broad smile crossing her face. "Still as beautiful as ever. What's it been? Five years?"

"Six. The anniversary was just a few days ago."

The smile that graced her face slipped a little. "Oh, sweet child." She hugged me again. "I'm so sorry."

"Sharla?"

"Over here, Mary. Come see who I found."

"Regina-bellina. Oh, my goodness. How are you?"

I was passed from one set of arms to another, like a *bocce* ball being tossed between two team players. These arms belonged to Sharla's twin in every way except skin color. They were the same age, had the same hair style, even wore dresses along the same lines. But where Sharla's skin bespoke her African ancestry, Mary's skin was snow white, as was her hair, both gifts from her Scandinavian DNA.

"Girl, it's been too long," she said.

"I just told her the same thing."

"What are you doing here?" Mary asked, her gaze sliding over to Connor. "Are you with our angel, here?"

"Ladies." Connor bussed both their cheeks. "I'm glad you could come tonight."

"Are you kidding?" Sharla asked. "Like we'd ever miss one of your fundraisers."

"Especially when we get to take the final check home with us." Mary laughed.

"How do you know Regina?" he asked.

"The better question is how do you?"

Connor's ears went that adorable pink color at her question, her implication clear. "She made that fantastic cake over by the band for tonight."

Both woman turned to the dais.

"Child, you did that?" Sharla asked. "I don't remember you being a baker."

"I wasn't. Then. I went to pastry school...after."

I didn't need to tell these two after what. They knew the details of my life six years ago intimately, since they'd been so heavily involved in the day-to-day care of my daughter.

Back then Sharla and Mary had been the primary nurses assigned to Angie's care. Sharla was the day nurse, Mary her evening/nighttime one. They'd taken as much care of me as they had my daughter, always bringing me something to eat from the cafeteria because

I refused to leave Angie's bedside, or bringing in a sleep chair so I could spend the precious nights I had left with her and not have to go home.

"Ladies?"

Both nurses looked at me as if asking permission. I was the one who answered him, though. "Sharla and Mary were the nurses who took care of my daughter while she was at Pearl's Place."

"The most beautiful angel you ever saw," Sharla said, taking my hand.

Connor's eyes widened, his head bouncing back and forth between them and me.

"Wait? What? Your daughter? I didn't know you had a daughter."

"She…passed away. Six years ago."

"Six years? I'm confused. I thought your husband died six years ago."

"Johnny? No, he's not dead. Not that I know of anyway." You never know with Pop. "He's just gone. He bolted right after we buried Angie."

Connor's handsome face grew very serious.

"I could have sworn you told me you lost your husband." He shook his head. "But your daughter was a patient at Pearl's Place?"

"For almost three months."

Three of the most difficult, worst months of my entire life. Seeing these two wonderful woman again brought all the sad memories back to the surface I'd pushed down deep inside me just so I could start to function and live again. Sorrow flooded through my system as the horror of Angie's last days began pelting the front of my memory.

Her beautiful raven hair, gone, from the massive

chemotherapy, her tiny head encased in a pink turban aunt Frankie's mom, Nonna Constanza, had knitted to keep her warm. The veins visible just underneath her fragile skin, giving her a bluish, waxy hue. Her poor lips had been swollen, dry, and caked with scabs from the thrush caused by the never-ending rounds of antibiotics to help fight all the infections her little immune-compromised body fell victim to. No amount of lip balm or moisturizer helped heal them.

She'd stopped eating, stopped talking, stopped interacting with us until her lungs finally stopped and she was put on a ventilator. Five days later, her heart followed and there was nothing more to do.

"And now you're a baker?" Mary asked.

With a nod, I said, "I have my own bakery. It's called Angie's."

Both women shot each other a look.

"Oh, child."

Mary rubbed my back while Sharla, who still held my hand, squeezed it. Her kind voice was tinged with sadness, and I had to bite down on the inside of my cheek so I wouldn't make a fool of myself and let go the tears that had been threatening since they recognized me. I looked over at Connor, sending a silent plea for him to save me once again from emotions too difficult for me to contain. Unfortunately, he was prevented from coming to my rescue. Another tuxedoed man had come up to him, whispered something to him and then pointed to the dais.

Connor nodded, his eyes staying trained on me the entire time.

"Ladies, I'm sorry. I need a minute."

"That man is a saint," Sharla said when he'd left

us. "Do you have any idea how much money he raises for us each year?"

"Last year he donated a new MRI machine on top of the hundred thousand dollars he raised at this same event," Mary added.

My eyes tracked him all the way to the dais where he was met by his mother and a man who looked vaguely familiar. He was facing slightly away from me, but there was something in the shape of his head, the line of his chin that reminded me of someone. When he shook Connor's hand and then turned to face the crowd, I went stone still. Sharla still held my hand and must have felt the way my body reacted.

"Oh, Reggie, I'm sorry. I forgot Dr. Mendelsohn was here, too. He's on the board of directors now, and he's the one who accepts the funds donated for the center."

Garrison Mendelsohn hadn't changed much since the last time I'd seen him. Still holding himself ramrod straight as if, as Pop had commented more times than I could recall, he had a stick shoved up his bony ass. His stark white hair seemed a little thinner on top, his cheeks maybe a bit sunken. But he still looked like the arrogant, unfeeling man who'd whirled into Angie's room and pronounced her dead without ever offering any consolation or recognizing the family grief that surrounded my daughter's bedside.

He'd come, listened to her chest, then turned the alarm off the screaming ventilator. He'd pushed his glasses up on his beak-like nose, turned to us, and declared, "She's gone."

That was it. Then he left the room.

What happened after that was as vivid and clear in

my mind right now as it had been that horrible day. I'd flown from the room and pummeled his back, striking him, yelling at the top of my lungs at him, railing like *una donna pazza*—a crazy woman. It had taken two of my brothers and my father to pull me off of him. I'd broken his glasses and given him a black eye in the wake of it. Why he'd never pressed charges against me for assault I never knew. If I had to harbor a guess, Pop had somehow smoothed everything over as only he can.

Seeing Mendelsohn again now blew that last day of my daughter's life back into my mind as if I was watching a digital replay of it.

Suddenly, I couldn't breathe. In the next instant, my lungs hyper-inflated with air and my pulse started hammering in my chest. Sweat soaked my uniform coat like a bucket of water had been thrown over my head.

I had to leave. Now. I had to get out of here. Just like that day at Rockefeller Center, everything was closing in on me.

"Excuse me," I said to Sharla and Mary as I all but ran from the room. I heard them calling my name, but I ignored the sound.

Down the long hallway and through the main part of the restaurant, until I passed the reservation podium, I ran. Once out on the avenue, I chugged in a huge breath and bent forward, hands on my knees.

Home. I needed to get home.

I shot my hand in the air when I saw a cab approaching, its light on, and poured into it when it pulled to the curb. I gave my address and then collapsed back on the seat.

Chapter 6

Regina's tips for surviving in a big Italian family:
6. Never be late for church.

I barely made it up the stairs to my apartment before I slammed the door and fell back against it. My breathing was still loud and choppy, and it echoed in the empty space around me. It was a wonder I was still able to stand upright. Once I closed my eyes and began breathing in through my nose then pushing the air out through my mouth, I slowly, gradually, started to calm.

As soon as I knew I wouldn't drop to the floor in a pathetic heap, I pushed off the door, sat down at my kitchen table, and dropped my head in my hands.

Disgust galloped through me. I was such a coward, such a weakling, to have run from Mendelsohn when I should have confronted him and apologized for what I'd done six years ago. He wasn't the reason my daughter had died, but I'd lashed out at him, blaming him for her death. His bedside manner may have left a lot to be desired—a *whole* lot—but the entire time he'd been responsible for her medical care, he'd done everything in his power to keep her comfortable. And while he hadn't been able to save her from the ravages of the hateful disease, he had tried. Valiantly, I had to admit.

Tonight, I should have gone up to him and, with

those six years of separation and a lifetime of emotional growth behind me, thanked him for what he'd done for Angie.

But I hadn't. I'd bolted from the situation unable to face the tormented pain of my past. And worse, I'd left Connor in the lurch. He'd asked me to stay, to help him with the cake presentation, and I'd flown without an explanation. Not a very professional way to act. I should have been able to separate my emotions from my job, but I hadn't. Any idea of the two of us being together now was probably over. This was his big night, and I'd run away from it, selfishly unable to be supportive because of my own raw and painful memories.

Just when I'd opened my heart again to the possibility I could be happy, I'd sabotaged the opportunity. Tears crept down my cheeks filled with sadness at what might have been.

How long I sat at the table, my own little pity party consuming me, I haven't a clue. I didn't know I'd fallen asleep until I felt my phone buzzing in my uniform jacket pocket.

Connor's name danced across the screen.

There was no way I could talk to him, so I hit the ignore icon. Not two seconds later, I got a text.

I'm downstairs. Let me in.

I shot from the table to the window. True to his word, he was standing at my service entrance door, fresh snow raining down on him. His overcoat was pulled tight around his neck, his head and hands, bare. He glanced up and waved.

Everything in me said to send him away. To just leave things as they were. I was mortified to face him, ashamed at my behavior.

Everything, but my heart.

There really was no decision to make, no choice to choose. I ran down the stairs at breakneck speed and unlocked the door. Freezing cold air and tufts of snow swirled around him like a tornado as he came in. Before I could shut the door, he pulled me into his arms and kicked it closed with his foot.

"Regina."

My name on his lips was gruff and filled with deep worry. His body shook against mine, and I knew it wasn't because he was cold.

"Why did you leave?" he asked, his mouth pressed against my hair. "I looked up and saw you bolting from the room. I wanted to go after you, but I couldn't get away. Not then."

He pulled me an arm's length away, his gaze dragging over my face. Twin lines of concern fluted his forehead as the corners of his eyes grew tight. "I was frantic something had happened to you."

I dropped my chin, afraid he'd see the shame in my eyes.

"Look at me," he commanded. "Please."

When I did my face was wet with tears. Connor's warm, gentle hands cupped my chin and swiped at my cheeks with the pads of his thumbs. The gesture almost dropped me to my knees again. "Sweetheart, talk to me. Tell me what happened. Why did you leave?"

He was such a good man. From everything I'd seen with my own eyes, I knew this to be true. He deserved the truth. Resigned to that, I nodded.

"Let's go upstairs. I need…I need a cup of tea."

He held my hand the entire time and only let go

once we were in my kitchen. While the water came to a boil in my teapot, I took down two mugs from the cabinet, poured milk into the creamer.

After shucking his wet coat and hanging it up on the peg by the door, Connor slipped out of his tuxedo jacket, sat at the kitchen table, and silently watched me set up everything. The top button of his shirt was popped open, the bow tie undone and hanging from the confines of the collar. He'd swiped his snow-damp hair back from his forehead to slick it down the sides as it had been earlier in the evening. With the tea steeping, I brought the mugs to the table and sat.

Connor stirred his tea and, after I'd taken my first few sips, asked, "Better?"

I nodded and kept my hands woven around the hot mug. The heat went a long way to helping to calm my nerves.

"Talk to me."

I took a breath, trying to figure out how to explain why I'd left without sounding like an emotional wreck—which is what I'd been and still was.

"First, I have to apologize for running away. It was never my intent. I'd promised you I'd stay and cut the cake, so I'm sorry I left you to handle it all."

He shrugged. "It got taken care of."

"Oh, good." I drank some more tea. Focused what I wanted to say.

"Seeing Sharla and Mary was a bit of a shock and, I have to admit, made me a little sad. But I thought I could handle it without breaking down. Those two got me through so many horrible days, you have no idea. They are simply two of the kindest people I've ever met." I sighed. "But when I saw you with Dr.

Mendelsohn, well, it became too much for me."

"Why?"

I looked across the table at him. His face was so caring, so open. My heart melted a little at the natural kindness of this man.

"He was the doctor in charge of my daughter's care while she was at Pearl's Place. He…let's just say we didn't part well."

"Don't do that, Regina. Don't brush over anything. Tell me what happened between the two of you. All of it. About your daughter, your husband. Everything."

"There's not that much to tell."

"Regina."

I nodded again.

I explained first about Johnny and me. The shame I'd felt for so many years about the reason we needed to get married still dragged deep. I wasn't the first girl on the planet to ever walk down the aisle with a baby bump camouflaged under a frilly wedding gown, but I *was* the first in my strict, Italian, Catholic, and overprotective family to do so. The embarrassment of that fact never quite went away, always lurking somewhere near the surface, ready to be used as verbal ammunition if a family fight occurred. Not that it ever had been. My mother saw to that. But still, the shame lingered.

Connor, though, accepted what I told him without showing any judgment or disapproval in his features.

"He never wanted to get married. Who could blame him, really. He never got the chance to go to college. At eighteen, he was saddled with a pregnant teenaged wife. But with the baby coming, he did the right thing. We were okay for a few years. While it might not have been the life Johnny pictured for himself, he adored Angelina. She was everything to him. I'd named her after my *nonna,* and she was true to her name."

"Angel?"

"Yeah."

I got up and went into my bedroom.

"This was taken about three months before she started to get noticeably sick. The doctors told us the tumor in her brain had been growing for a while before we ever saw any signs of it."

I handed him the framed photograph Johnny had snapped of the two of us. We were in Central Park during the fall, sitting on a bench near the pond. Angelina's two top teeth had come out a few days before, and her wide, toothless grin dominated her face. She was sitting on my lap, my arms around her tiny waist as I peeked over her shoulder my own huge smile in place.

"She's your clone," Connor said, his gaze ping-ponging between me and the photograph.

"Everyone said that. She didn't did have any of Johnny in her at all. Not in looks. Not in disposition."

He handed the frame back to me. "You said she had a brain tumor?"

"Glioblastoma." I shook my head and sat back down. "I know it's ridiculous to hate a word, but I hate that one. With every ounce of my soul."

He reached across the table and took one of my hands with his. A feeling of safety, of acceptance, of warm promise, seeped through my skin at his touch.

"At first, she kept knocking into walls, and her whole perspective on her surroundings seemed off. We chalked it up to a growth spurt. My nephews were like that. One minute they were natural athletes, the next they were tripping over their feet. A week later their pants were too short and then everything righted again. Only it never righted with Angie."

I took a few sips of my tea, my free hand still in Connor's, his eyes still on me.

"She'd always been an enthusiastic reader, and she read early. A benefit of being an only child: she got all the attention focused on her. One day, she put down the book she was flipping through and said, 'Mama, the words are swimming.' I figured she needed glasses, so I took her to an optometrist. He told us to go to an ophthalmologist and made an appointment for us, but he wouldn't tell us why, just that she needed a specialist. We went, and the doc dilated Angie's eyes. After he examined her, he suggested we take her to her pediatrician. Again, he weren't told why."

"Isn't that illegal?" Connor asked. "Well, not illegal. That's the wrong word. But shouldn't they have told you what they suspected, or at least given you a heads-up?"

"You would think so. I don't know why they kept what they thought was wrong with her from us. Maybe they didn't want to scare us because they weren't sure. I don't know. Anyway, the pediatrician got us right in. After his examination, he called a pediatric oncologist, another two words I despise. Luckily, this doctor was part of the same practice, so we got right in to see him as well. Two MRIs and a boatload of other tests later and the diagnosis came down. Glioblastoma, stage four. Inoperable. Incurable."

"Jesus."

"She had three months of radiation to try and

shrink the tumor. Despite that, it continued to grow. The doctors said it was an all-invasive, rapidly growing cancer, and the more we weakened her immune system with the treatments, the faster the tumor would take over. We were referred to Pearl's Place by one of the oncology nurses at the hospital when Angie started physically deteriorating to where she needed continual around-the-clock medical and nursing care. Palliative care, it's called."

He nodded. "How long from diagnosis until..."

"A little under a year. She died on December tenth."

"The day I found you at Rockefeller Center."

I took another sip of my tea. The steam billowed over my face, coating it in warmth.

"What happened with Dr. Mendelsohn that made you so upset tonight? Was it just seeing him again? It all rushed back to you?"

"Partly. I told you we didn't end on the best of notes." Quickly, I explained what happened after Angie died.

"I know my anger was displaced. *Now*. Back then?" I shrugged and shook my head again. "I blamed him for not saving her and for being so cold and unfeeling when she died."

"Misplaced though it may have been, I think your anger was justified."

"Maybe." I brought a box of cookies I'd made the day before to the table, took one and offered him the box. "I have an aunt. Aunt Gracie. She's not my flesh and blood aunt, really my mother's sister-in-law's sister. Follow?"

"Got it."

"Afterward, months later after Angie was…buried, when I was able to function again, Aunt Gracie said something to me that I'd never considered. Something that made me feel guilty about the incident with Mendelsohn."

"What?"

"She said he probably acted the way he did, cold and detached, because he dealt with dying children every day. No one gets better at Pearl's Place, she said. It's the place sick kids go to die. Their last stop before Heaven. He probably acted the way he did because if he ever really thought about it, he wouldn't be able to cope, to function, to do his job. Who would, she asked, knowing that every day when you went to work you couldn't prevent a child from dying? You had to watch them and their families suffer, knowing the ultimate end was always the same. That had to weigh on his soul. Heavily."

"I think she's right."

"I do, too. When I saw him tonight, I should have gone up to him to apologize, not run away like a coward."

"I don't think that word can be used to describe you, Regina." He squeezed my hand and stood, still holding it. He squatted down in front of me and took my other hand. "You're the strongest, bravest woman I think I've ever met."

"I'm not brave."

"You are. You could have told me to go to Hell when you found out why I wanted the cake made, what it was for. Said 'no way' and then kicked me out the door. But you didn't. You agreed, even knowing how much it might dredge up old and horrible memories.

That's brave in my book. In anyone's."

I wanted to believe that, I really did. I'd tried to tell myself the reason I'd agreed to make the cake in the first place was because I knew it was time to move on from it all. To try and forget.

Memories can't be lost, though, just tucked away until something comes along to spark them to life again.

Connor tugged on my hands, bringing me to my feet. As he stared down at me, he wound his arms around my waist and pulled me up against him.

"Thank you for telling me. All of it."

"I'm so sorry I ran out on you. I promised to stick around and help. Now, in addition to feeling like a fool for letting my emotions get the better of me, I feel guilty I left you to take care of it."

"Like I said, no worries there." One corner of his lips pulled up. "Sharla and Mary, willingly helped by Uncle Aiden, took care of it along with the staff. The cake, like I knew it would be, was a huge hit. Before it was cut and served, every phone in the place was aimed at it snapping pictures. Don't be surprised if you start trending on social media tomorrow."

For the first time in hours, I smiled. Really smiled. Just being with him seemed to chase all the sadness, all the worry, away.

"There it is," Connor said, his voice low, pleasure flowing through it.

This time I knew what he was referring to.

"Thank you," I said. "For listening. For understanding. I never talk about this. Never. Any of it. It felt good to tell someone."

He kissed the tip of my nose. "I'm glad you did. That you trusted me enough to."

Trust. A five-letter word that meant so much more than its simple definition. For so long, so many years, I'd kept to myself, unable and unwilling to reach out and try to find love, knowing I couldn't take the chance my heart wouldn't get broken again. Even though I'm strong, and like the elder females in my family tell me often, I'm a San Valentino, I knew I wouldn't be able to withstand another heartbreak. So I took care of myself, my business, and my family, allowing no one to enter into that circle.

Connor was the only person I'd every told about Angie and Johnny who wasn't related to me. For whatever reason, I *did* trust him with my memories. And, I realized, with my heart.

I reached up and cupped his cheek with my hand. With a tiny shift of his chin, Connor burrowed into my palm and kissed it, his gaze staying glued to mine.

His fingers began drawing tiny circles along the curve in my back. I swear on the rosary beads Nonna received when she made her Communion and which now sat in my purse, willed to me after her death, that each little trace and trail sent a shockwave through my entire body. Desire for this man, for his touch, shattered through me.

I lifted up on my toes and pressed my lips against his warm ones. His breath exhaled in one long, sweet sigh.

Yeah, I know just how you feel.

When I slid my fingers up over his marble-hard chest, past his perfect jaw, to link behind his neck, his shoulders relaxed against my hands. His own fingers stopped their subtle seductive dance at my waist, and he flattened his palms against me, pushing me so close there wasn't a whisper of room between our bodies. Every cut, curved, carved inch of him was pressed against me, and *mio Dio*, I wanted to be closer still. And by closer, I mean skin to skin.

Yeah, I know. But even good little Italian girls can have frustrated, sexy thoughts. Even *needs*.

I'd been intimate with one other man my entire life, and let's face it, neither one of us considered the other their soul mate. Sex had scratched an itch between us but had never been the fireworks exploding, *la piccolo morte*—little death—it was rumored to be. We were married, so we had sex. Easy and comfortable sex.

Standing in my living room kissing and being kissed by Connor Gilhooly, I wanted more than easy and comfortable. I wanted the explosion, the notion that being with this person was going to be the be all and end all a true romantic connection was supposed to be. And I wanted it with him.

Before I could form the words in my mind to ask him, Connor scooped me up in his arms and walked backward with me toward my couch. He plopped us both down, me on top of his lap, and we both laughed at the creaking sound my couch springs made from our weight.

I slung one hand around his shoulders, laid the other over his chest. Against my hand, his heart raced like a speeding locomotive aiming straight for the finish line. He lifted it and brought it to his lips. Such an old-world gesture, so romantic, so endearing.

I simply melted.

"Regina."

I tilted my head. "How come you don't call me Reggie like everyone else? You always address me by my proper name. How come?"

He took the hand he held and rubbed the back of it against his cheek.

Did I say melted? Turned into molten lava—boiling hot and explosive—is more the truth.

"Queen," he said against my hand. "Your name means queen."

"I know. Although I think it's more like *queenly woman*."

He shook his head. "Queen. That's what you are." He let go of my hand, and his drifted across to cup the back of my neck. He gave a gentle tug, pulling my face a hair's width from his. With a look I can only call *wanting,* he added, "My queen," right before he kissed me again.

Emotions and sensations slammed through me shooting straight up from my core. With a frenzied expectation, his tongue swiped at my lips and with expert determination parted them and mated with my own.

Every single nip and suck and swipe shot little bullets of sexual frenzy straight down to the part of me sitting in his lap. Restless, needful, blind with frustration, I began squirming and writhing against him. When I felt the solid hard length of him grow and roll beneath me, I pressed down more firmly.

We both groaned loudly enough for the sound to echo in my apartment.

"God, Regina. You feel like heaven," he whispered in my ear and then sucked my lobe between his teeth.

"You do, too."

Gesu. Was that breathless, throaty voice really mine? It was a cross between Marilyn Monroe—Pop's all-time favorite movie star—and Kathleen Turner, Ma's favorite actress.

Once again our lips met. I knew his taste now, the feel of him, his very essence, as if I'd kissed him every day of my life. As if I fell asleep in his arms and woke up the same way. In his arms, I felt cherished and wanted, two things I'd never felt with my ex.

Connor kissed me with possession and passion in every swirl of his tongue, every glide of his lips against my skin.

After a long while, I laid my head down on his shoulder, nuzzled the space under his ear, and breathed him in.

Connor exhaled a long, slow breath. Cuddled together, he kissed my temple. "Can I ask you something?" he said when his breathing slowed a bit.

"Anything."

"Has there been anyone in your life since your divorce? Any guy you…cared about?"

I sat back up so I could see his face. I'd been thinking my heart was open to falling in love again, but when I saw Connor's expression—a little nervous, a little vulnerable, and a whole pasta-bowl full of desirable male—the thought my heart was opening again flew. It was already open—wide—and filled with Connor.

"The only man ever in my life was my husband," I confessed. "Since Angie's death, and then my divorce, I haven't dated or been interested in any man, despite the well-intentioned, crazy efforts of my family."

His grin was lopsided and adorable. I ran a finger along his bottom lip, slightly swollen from kissing me so thoroughly. He sucked it between his teeth and gently bit down. That little nip shunted down my spine all the way to my toes.

"There hasn't been anyone I felt I wanted to be with."

He tilted his head, his stormy gaze trained on me.

I swallowed the lump in my throat and set my heart free. "Until now."

Those storm clouds cleared, brightened, and grew soft.

He pulled my head back to his shoulder and ran his lips across my temple. A sigh filled with so much emotional release glided from deep inside him. "You can't possibly know what that means to me," he said.

A sense of complete contentment drifted through me. I closed my eyes, my head on his shoulder, my hand on his chest, the feel of his heart beating under my fingers once again.

Not only contentment, I thought, but happiness as well.

And…love.

****

Something warm was heating my cheeks. I shifted and opened my eyes. I was in my bed, bright sunshine streaming in through the window across from it.

Morning.

I had no idea how I'd gotten here. My last, clear, before-morning-caffeine memory was of sitting on the couch with Connor, talking and cuddling.

Connor. Just the thought of him made me smile. We'd talked for hours the night before, interspersed with periods of such intense and hot—and by hot, I mean *burning*—kissing sessions that my lips still felt tingly and satisfied. The man was a world-class master of the art of making love to a pair of lips.

I sat up, tossed the covers off, and glanced down. I was still completely dressed. My shoes were sitting on the floor next to the dresser. Connor must have carried me to my bed before leaving. A quick glance at my bedside clock and I nearly had a heart attack.

8:15 a.m.

Madonna. Pop was going to be here any minute to pick me up for Sunday Mass.

I shot up from the bed and ran into my bathroom. I'm a world-class speed shower-taker. It comes from living with four brothers who, during their teenage years, defined the term narcissist, spending hours in the bathroom each morning as they got ready for school, and then later on, work. In less than three minutes, I was washed and dressed for church.

I sprinted to my living room and had the second almost-coronary of the morning. Connor was sitting at my kitchen table, a mug in his hands, another one on the table across from him. His tuxedo was rumpled and wrinkled. A dark swatch of morning scruff slid across his chiseled jaw and cheeks, and my fingertips tingled with longing to run them across it. His hair was no longer slicked back at his temples but fell again in its natural state across his brow. He looked totally at ease and effortlessly natural sitting in my chair, as if he woke every morning clad in a tuxedo, ready to face the day.

"I heard the shower go on, so I knew you were up," he said, his mouth lifting in one corner. He nodded at the steaming mug on the table. "I made you tea. I didn't see any coffee in the cabinets, so I figured you drank it in the morning."

"You spent the night?"

He nodded. "You need a new couch."

"Why?"

"Because there's at least one spring that's died. Maybe more." He cocked his head right, then left. "I may need a massage today to work the kinks out."

"No, I mean, why did you stay?"

He put his mug down on the table and reached out a hand to me. Slowly, I walked around the table, stopped in front of him, and took it. With one small tug, he had me on his lap.

"I didn't want to leave you alone after you fell asleep."

"Why not?"

He lifted one shoulder. "I just didn't. You'd had a pretty emotional evening. I thought I should stay close in case you needed anything."

What would he have thought if I'd told him all I really needed was him?

"You carried me to bed?"

"Yes. You never even batted an eye, you were so deeply asleep." With a chuckle he added, "If I hadn't known why, my poor ego would have been bruised at your falling asleep while we were…together."

I swiped at the fringe cross his brow. "And you took off my shoes?"

He nodded again and grinned. "I didn't think you slept in them."

I grinned back at him. "Not as a rule. And that's not the first time I've slept in my work clothes, either."

He lifted his mug and had a sip while he held me.

"You didn't have to spend an uncomfortable night on the couch, Connor. You could have crawled in next to me to sleep."

Something in his eyes changed. Those wispy cloud colors morphed into smoldering smoke and ash as hunger glazed through them, and *mio Dio*, I wanted to be the one to feed him. And by feed him—well, I don't think that needs an explanation.

With purposeful movements, he put the mug back down, his gaze never leaving mine, and said, "As lovely an invitation as that is, when I…sleep…with you the first time, Regina, I want you to be awake."

Oh, holy and sweet *bambino Gesu.*

I swallowed the *bocce* ball in my throat, the sound so loud there was no way he couldn't hear it. "I…I…"

Never in my life had I been speechless. There's no such word in my Italian family's lexicon. Words trip off our tongues like pebbles roll down a hill.

But that statement, one of fact for sure, turned me mute.

That little corner lift of his lips drifted up higher as his hand nudged me a little closer. "Now, you've been awake for five minutes, and I still haven't gotten a good morning kiss."

Ma and Pop didn't raise a fool. And Connor didn't need to ask me twice.

I settled my hands on his shoulders, marveling once again at how strong, solid, and powerful they felt, and, with a grin, leaned in.

The slam of the downstairs door had me pulling back and jumping off his lap.

"What's wrong?"

"It's my father. He's here to pick me up for church. Quick." I yanked on his arm, pulling him up. "Go hide in the bedroom so he doesn't see you. You can slip out after we leave."

"Why?"

"Don't ask. Just please, please. Go." I tried to shove him from the room, but do you know how difficult it is to shove two hundred pounds of non-complying male anywhere? I'm strong, but Connor is built like a tank. Add that he'd rooted his feet to the floor, and I had no chance of propelling him anywhere he didn't want to go.

"Regina, what's wrong—"

He was cut off when my father blew through the front door of my apartment, bringing cold air with him and swiping snow from his hat and shoulders.

Now before you ask why he has the key to *my* apartment, remember, he owns the building and, in effect, is my landlord. If your next statement is that doesn't give him the right to burst in on me and invade my privacy, I'll counter, *have you met my father*? *Mia famiglia?* Personal privacy is as alien a concept to them as little green men from Mars.

"*Madonna.* It's cold out today," Pop declared as he tugged his hat off and looked up at me.

And stopped in his tracks.

"Pop. You're early." My voice was a bit too loud and bright for the scene I knew was playing in front of his eyes.

"Regina Maria?"

Uh-oh. Pop never addressed me by my full name unless I was in deep, deep *merda.*

His gaze slid to Connor. I watched as it took in the scruff on his face, the way he was dressed, the nonchalant way Connor'd stuck his hands into his pants pockets.

131

"Irish. This is a...surprise."

"Mr. San Valentino." He glanced at me. "I'll let myself out, Regina, so you two can get to Mass. Thanks again for last night."

"*What?*"

My shoulders met my ears at the hit from the bellowing sound. My father's roar is legendary in our family, and whenever he lets it out, the wisest choice is to run.

Unfortunately, I didn't have that choice right now.

Before I could say a word, Connor, God bless him, came to my defense. In a calm voice and with a smooth smile, he told Pop, "Your daughter is a lifesaver, Mr. San Valentino. She baked a magnificent cake for a fundraiser I had last night. The entire place was amazed by how it looked and the delicious way it tasted."

"You know, Pop. The one for Pearl's Place?"

His skeptical brow quirked as his gaze popped from me to Connor and then back to settle on me.

"Yeah," he said. "Yeah. I remember. But what are you doing—"

I knew the direction that question was going, so I pulled an old teenage trick out of my pocket that my cousin Chloe used to use on her parents: I diverted his attention.

"Pop, we're gonna be late." I grabbed Connor's coat from the peg and shoved it at him. "You're welcome for the cake. I'm glad everything turned out okay."

God bless him again, because he got the hint, took it, and ran with it. Literally. Within a second of shrugging into his coat, he tossed my father a wave and sprinted down the stairs.

Before I could get the third degree from my father, I grabbed my own coat and, hustling him out of the apartment, said, "Come on. Ma's in the car, right?" I steamrolled right over his answer before he could start grilling me like fresh fish about why Connor was in my apartment this morning if the event I'd baked for had been the previous night. "Let's get going. I don't want to get tossed a grumpy *malocchio* from Father Mario if we walk in late."

I shoved the poor man out the door and down the stairs, chatting inanely the entire time about nothing at all. The last thing I wanted was ten thousand questions about Connor while we were on our way to church. Once we were in the car my mother started up with her plans for the holidays and talked nonstop until we arrived at St. Rita's. Pop's eyes flicked to the rearview mirror frequently, though, questions and concerns filling them.

Chapter 7

Regina's tips for surviving in a big Italian family:
7. Never let them see you sweat, and try to get the last
word during any argument.

My family takes their Catholicism very seriously. Despite the sometimes questionable business deals they get involved in, their faith is strong and practiced with devotion. As far as I know, they haven't broken any commandments—or laws—maybe just reinterpreted a few from time to time.

When I'd wound up pregnant and unmarried at seventeen, the first person my parents took me to wasn't our family doctor, but our parish priest. He was instrumental in setting up my quick marriage and skimming over several church dictates like marriage counseling and the posting of the banns. I'm pretty sure Pop made a hefty donation to the parish's refurbishing fund at the time, just like he did to the roof fundraising drive when it came time for my divorce from Johnny. Father Mario, our old-as-dirt pastor, is a long-time family friend and when it came time to bury Angelina, he was the one who said the funeral mass at St. Rita's and then accompanied us to the graveside to conduct her final blessing. He's said all the family's funeral masses, in fact, and my family views him as an honorary member.

Since Christmas is such a busy season for the church, Father Mario and his junior priest, Father Tom Santini, who also happens to be my cousin Gia's brother-in-law, were run ragged with all the weddings, funerals, baptisms, hospital visits, and masses they needed to perform daily.

"New guy's saying the mass," Ma said as she read the bulletin. Father Tom has been a member of our parish for almost a decade, but everyone still refers to him as "the new guy," and probably will until Father Mario takes the express train to the pearly gates.

We all squeezed into three pews like sardines in a can. I sat next to my mother and father with my oldest brother and his family. Behind us, the rest of my brothers and their families had settled in. In the pews in front of us, my uncle Joey, aunt Frankie, and all their kids and families sat, whispering. Across the aisle, Aunt Frankie's sisters and their husbands packed into two shorter pews. Aunt Grace had a cold, evidenced by her loud goose-honking cough every few seconds and then the deep, rumbling clearing of the phlegm from way down in the back her throat. The disgusting sound echoed straight up to the church rafters, bounced off the statues of Christ and the Holy Family in the crèche, and then sandblasted the congregation with the mucousy grumble.

"She should-a stayed home," Ma said, shooting a squinty-eyed *malocchio* at her sister-in-law's sister. "She's gonna infect everybody around her, and right before the holidays, too." She muttered something in Italian, and it didn't take a genius to realize it was a curse. Immediately after she closed her lips, she made the sign of the cross and tossed the statue of Christ that sat over the altar a pleading, sorrowful look. I knew she was asking for forgiveness for casting a curse in God's house.

Mia famiglia. Sigh.

The organist sounded, and like the good and respectful Catholics we are, we all rose. Father Tom stepped through the sacristy door with two altar boys, the reader, and the cantor in front of him. Eddie, one of my cousins, carried the fifty-pound, four-foot, gold-encrusted cross and led the procession down the center aisle of the church.

"Frankie and Joey's Eddie is applying to the Knights," Ma whispered to Pop. My mother's whisper is the kind that's euphemistically called a stage whisper, because everyone in a forty-foot radius can hear it. "You should-a joined years ago when you was asked," she added, her pursed lips pointing to my father.

"The Knights of Columbus take up too much time," Pop said back. No whisper for him. "I was busy back then with the business and couldn't spare the time. The Knights meet, like, twice a week. Sometimes more if there's an event."

In full disclosure here, I've never really known exactly what my father does for a living, what he calls, *his business.* I've heard him described as an entrepreneur by some, a wheeler-dealer by others. But there's always been food on the table, a new family car for Christmas each year, and a roof bought and paid for in cash over our heads, so I never gave it much consideration.

"Excuses," Ma countered. "You could join now. You need all the help you can to get into Heaven."

To that, Pop just shook his head and rolled his eyes.

While the procession, well, *proceeded*, up to the altar, Gracie's hacking and throat clearing accompanied them, drowning out the organist and the singer.

From my position, I saw my Aunt Frankie turn in her sister's direction and make some motion to her. I just bet it was for her to either quiet the noise or leave.

As the procession passed us, we all genuflected and made the sign of the cross.

Once Father Tom was situated and the Mass began, I let my mind drift to Connor.

To say I was smitten would be an understatement. The man hit most of the boxes on my what-you-want-in-a-guy list, not that I'd ever actually made the list or referred to it. He was smart. Check. Successful. Check. Good-looking. Double check. Kind, courteous, and loved his family. Check, check, check. The one box I couldn't check was his nationality. While it made no difference to me whether or not he had Italian blood coursing through him, it did matter to my parents. They'd gone on and endlessly on when my brothers were younger about finding brides who matched them in social status, religion, and ancestry.

I was the one child who'd defied that. Johnny had a German father and a Spanish mother. At the time, I didn't care about the differences in our backgrounds. Once we were married and had to actually live under the same roof, those cultural differences became apparent. Johnny had watched his mother kowtow and bend to his father's will throughout their marriage, and he expected me to behave the same way. Not happening. I mean, have you met the women in my family? All strong willed, opinionated, and mouthy. It's coded into our DNA.

Connor's mother had a lovely and refined way about her but wasn't snooty or a nose-pincher, a term my mother uses to explain how someone looks down their nose at you. Their nostrils flare at the tip while the bridge of their nose looks pinched and pained while they size you up.

I hadn't met his father, but if he was anything like Aiden, the man was sure to be a darling.

Unfortunately, no matter how darling or charming or nice I thought a man was—and Connor hit all three—my parents were never going to accept any man for me that they didn't vet completely. They had their own man-list for what I needed, and the most important box to be checked on it was that the guy came from an Italian background and put family first.

A long-winded hack and then a deep nose suck blew through my thoughts from across the aisle. This time my mother's *malocchio* was joined by my other aunts and all the wives of my brothers and cousins. It was a wonder Grace didn't petrify on the spot, like Lot's wife, from all the angry squinted glances zeroed in on her.

I think Father Tom even tossed her a stink eye.

Once the final blessing was spoken and Father Tom was stationed at the front door of the church to shake hands and give blessings, my family nudged and wedged their way to him.

From behind me, Aunt Frankie said in a voice that also didn't know the meaning of whisper, "Gracie, you should-a stayed home instead of infectin' the whole congregation with ya germs."

A loud nose blow into a tissue and Grace glared at her older sister as she swiped at her reddened nostrils. "You'd-a come too if you was sick, and you know it, Francesca. It's nine days 'til Christmas. I can't be skipping church on account of I gotta cold."

"You could try," my Uncle Joey murmured. Only it didn't come out like a murmur since everyone in the next six pews heard him.

My cousin Gia and her husband, Tim, Father Tom's twin brother, made their way up to the priest, then kissed him on both cheeks. My father envied his older brother because Joey had a son-in-law with a priest for a brother, and therefore—in his thoughts—a direct link to God. To see Tom and Tim together was a little scary at times. They were monozygotic, or identical, twins. The only way I'd ever been able to tell them apart was because Tom always wore his clerical collar. Always. Every family event he'd ever been a guest at he wore his full uniform. If he hadn't, I would have a hard, if not impossible, time telling the brothers from one another.

As a unit, my family made their way up to the junior priest, shook hands, and received a blessing. Then we all headed back to my parents' house for the usual Sunday food fest, or as my brothers referred to it, the best meal they got all week, since none of their wives were the cooks Ma was.

My mother had been slow-cooking a pork roast all morning, and by the time we got home and were ready to sit down to eat, it was done to perfection.

After grace, my father turned his attention away from the conversation my brothers were having about the Jets, and toward me.

"What's going on with you and that Irish guy?" he asked without any preamble.

Luckily, I hadn't taken a sip from the water glass I'd lifted to my mouth, otherwise I knew I would have choked on the liquid.

"Nothing."

"Regina Maria."

"Really, Pop. Nothing. I made a cake for him. That's it."

I could hear the angels in Heaven tsk-tsking me. I'd been in church less than two hours ago, and now I was committing a sin by lying to my father. I could see a visit to the confessional before the end of the day was in order.

"Guys you make cakes for don't usually spend the night in your apartment, little girl."

My brother knows a guy named Tony Cartieri. Everyone who knows him agrees that if Tony didn't have bad luck, he'd have no luck.

Right at the moment Pop made that statement, I knew exactly how old Tony felt, because the conversation had slowed and ebbed, Pop's words spreading around the table loud and clear. The kids were set up in the living room, so I don't think they got wind of it. But everyone else did.

Ten pair of eyes glared at me from all corners of the table. Some were wide-eyed; some were narrowed. All of them were filled with varying levels of emotions ranging from shocked (Ma) to suspicious (my brothers) to pleased (my sisters-in-law).

"Regina." Ma threw her napkin on her plate and slammed her cutlery next to her plate. "What is your father talking about? What man spent the night at your apartment?"

"It's not like it sounds, Ma. It was late and we were talking, and then we both just fell asleep—"

"*Holy Madonna.*" She made the sign of the cross and closed her eyes, hands clasped together as her lips moved silently in prayer.

"Where?" 'Carlo asked.

"Where what?"

"Where did the two of you fall asleep? In your bed?"

Another finger cross from Ma. This time she kissed her fingertips afterward and threw a prayer up to the Lord.

"I don't think you get to ask me that question, 'Carlo. I'm thirty-two years old, and you're my brother, not my father."

"What I am is suspicious," he spat back. "How come we didn't know you were seeing a guy? Why you keeping him a secret?"

"First of all, what I do in the privacy of my own home"—now Ma was rocking back and forth as she prayed—"or don't do, is none of your business. Second, I'm not seeing anyone, so the fact that it's a secret is null and void. Stop with the third degree, GianCarlo. Use it on your own kids, 'cause like I said, you're not my father."

"But I am," Pop said, his tone hard and filled with anger, "so answer it. Where did Irish sleep last night?"

"Irish?" Petey exclaimed. "What the Hell kinda name is that?"

"Language, Pietro," Ma said, awaking from her spiritual coma to chastise her son.

There are so many things I simply adore about my

family. The unshakeable connection and love we all have; the fact that we live close to one another; our shared faith and sense of tradition. But the one thing I do hate is the antiquated morality system they adhere to. Girls don't have sex with men before marriage, plain and simple. Of course since the one and only time I'd done just that, I'd wound up pregnant and forced to get married, my parents' concerns made sense.

To them.

I was almost fifteen years older, much wiser, and a full-fledged adult now, but I was still treated like an ignorant *bambina* who had to be protected from wolves and scoundrels. If my father had his way, I'd be married right now to one of his goombahs, eight months pregnant with probably our seventh child, and in the kitchen making gravy.

So many times over the years, I'd wanted to smack him on the back of the head much the way he smacks us, and say, "Wake up! It's twenty-first-century America, not eighteenth-century Sicily." Wanting to do something and actually doing it, though, are very different beasts.

So.

I don't get mad often, especially with my family, but I was tired, overworked, emotionally drained, and royally pissed off right now, so the anger bled through my usual calm.

I rose from my chair and threw my napkin down on the table like my mother had. "You know what? I'm done. I'm done with you all treating me like a child. I'm not one of your underlings, Pop, who needs to be kept on a short leash and told what to do every minute of the day because you don't have enough trust to let

them act on their own. And"—I glared at my brothers—
"I'm not five years old and unable to defend myself
against bullies and bad guys. You don't have to hold
my hand so I can cross the street and not get hit by a
car." I grabbed my plate and walked to the kitchen.
"I'm done with you all thinking I can't make a wise and
appropriate decision with my life," I added over my
shoulder. I placed the dish in the sink and called out,
"I'm done with the checking up on me, the second-
guessing me, and the way you all think you have a right
to manage my life."

I yanked my coat off the hall tree and yelled, "I'm
a thirty-two-year-old grown-ass woman who owns and
manages her own business and her own life. I don't
need protectors, handlers, or any of you telling me what
to do, who to see, or how to conduct myself. I've been
on my own a long time, and I think I've done a great
job with myself, even if you all don't." I shrugged into
my coat and wound my scarf around my neck. "If I
want a man to spend the night or not, it's none of your
damn business. Deal with it."

I may have screeched that last part.

I slammed the door behind me and sprinted down
the stairs of the brownstone, my ungloved hand waving
in the air for a passing cab.

As an exit line, I think it was a pretty good one.

Chapter 8

Regina's tips for surviving in a big Italian family: 8. Family means everything, so forgiveness is nonnegotiable.

The entire drive home, my phone blew up with texts and voice messages. The cabbie kept shifting his gaze to me in his rearview every time a new ping sounded. Furious with my entire family, I silenced the ring tones and alerts.

The second I walked through my apartment door, my house phone started ringing. If they couldn't get in touch with me via cell, they knew the old-fashioned princess phone that had belonged to Nonna was still serviceable and sitting in my living room. I yanked the cord from the wall, silencing the blaring ringer.

My body shook from head to toes with anger. Years of pent-up emotions and resentment whirled like a tornado through my system. I loved my brothers, of that there was no doubt, but right now I didn't like them one bit. I'd even go so far as to say I despised them. Who did they think they were, passing judgment on me and questioning me like I was criminal, or worse, one of Pop's wiseguy-wannabes?

I could understand my father acting like the alpha male in the group. He was. Plus, he was my father. I knew whatever he did, whatever questions he asked was because he loved me and wanted to make sure I was okay, not in trouble, financially sound, and emotionally fulfilled. While his way of expressing that concern may have been overbearing and archaic, it was still his right as a parent to voice his concern and ask his questions.

Not so my brothers. They had no right to question me about anything.

I pulled my clothes off and jumped into the shower, needing to physically cleanse myself. The hot jet-massage shower spray—a gift from a guy my father floated a loan to who owned a hardware store—went a long way in untying the knots in my shoulders and neck. As I doused myself, I realized I'd never answered 'Carlo's question about where Connor had slept last night. That parting shot about a man spending the night if I wanted him to might have given them all the idea I'd actually had sex with Connor.

If only I'd been so lucky.

Right now, hot, sweaty, no-excuses, no-questions-asked sex with a man I found undeniably desirable sounded pretty darn good to me.

As I was getting dressed again in my old culinary school sweats, I picked up my phone. Twenty-seven texts. Ten from Pop, two each from my brothers, and two more from each of my sisters-in-law. A single text had come in from Connor while I was in church. His was the sole one I opened.

Sorry about this morning and if it upset your dad seeing me in your apartment. If you were my daughter, I'd be upset at finding you alone with a man, too.

Upset didn't even begin to describe it.

I'm gonna be busy for the next two days, but can I

see you on the 19th? I'll bring dinner over to your place after the bakery closes, if that's okay. I know you're super busy this close to Christmas, and you might not want to go out. Just let me know. And mille grazie *for everything you did for the fundraiser. Best cake ever.*

How cute was it that he'd written his thanks in Italian? Ya gotta love Google translate.

I sent a quick reply text telling him it sounded great.

With the rest of the afternoon stretching before me now since I wasn't spending it at my parents' house like I usually did on a Sunday, I went down into the bakery and worked on a few of the special orders for the week. Exhaustion pushed me back to my apartment long after darkness fell.

A glance at my phone and no new family missives had come through. Good. They'd gotten the hint to leave me alone.

When I crawled into bed an hour later after heating up a quick bowl of Ma's minestrone, a pair of eyes the color of clouds over the ocean followed me into dreamland.

****

"Shit really hit the fan after you left yesterday, Zia Reggie," Pesce informed me the next morning when he found me in my office. "I don't think I've ever seen Nonno go after my dad like that before."

"Nonno was mad at 'Carlo?"

"Pissed beyond words. The minute you left, he started in on him how he shoulda kept his mouth shut about you and let him handle the Irish situation."

"That's what he called it? The Irish situation?"

Pesce tossed me one of his rare smiles. "Yeah.

Nonna sat there, saying the rosary the whole time they went back and forth. And when the uncles got involved, well, shit got super loud."

I could only imagine. "Was Nonna okay?"

He shrugged. "A little weepy. Ma and Aunt Penny took her to her bedroom and helped her lie down, all the while she was talking in Italian. Ma said she was saying the Hail Mary over and over."

No surprise there. She'd probably said two decades of the rosary while she'd been sitting at the table. I'd been prepared for a tongue-lashing this morning, or worse—the feared silent *malocchio*—when she arrived at work, but for the first time in the three years since the bakery had been open for business, she hadn't come in. My night crew manager, Terese, told me Ma had called early in the morning and said she was taking a sick day. I saw this for the ruse it was. My mother never went against anything my father told her to do. He'd probably insisted she stay home until I came around and capitulated with a personal apology for my behavior.

Not gonna happen. Not now, at least. I was still pissed, ultra busy with baking, and I had quarterly taxes due at the end of the month and needed to finish up with them. My mother, in my mind, deserved a day or two off, so I hoped she was sitting in her big recliner in the living room and watching soaps and talk shows all day long on the sixty-inch flat screen Pop got her. And by got, you know I mean it fell off a truck somewhere in Bayonne.

The rest of my family was on radio silence during the morning, something I was thrilled about. I didn't want to talk to anyone. I'd said my piece and meant every word of it.

When I ran up to my apartment to fix myself a quick lunch at noon, I found Penny and Trixie waiting for me at the top of the stairs.

They were dressed as if they were going out bar hopping. Skintight jeans ending in four inch stilettos, the absolute wrong footwear for the weather outside, and short little jackets that did nothing to protect them from the cold and wind, and everything to show off their narrow waists and ample breasts. Their hair was teased and sprayed with so much product, even a category-five tornado wouldn't move a hair of it from place. Both of them were in their mid to late forties and trying valiantly to look like they hadn't seen the front end of thirty yet.

Trixie appeared to have been voted the spokesperson.

"We brought lunch," she said, holding up a brown paper shopping bag. "And leftovers from yesterday."

"Do my parents know you're here? Or you husbands?" I asked.

They flicked a glance at one another and shook their heads.

"So this isn't some kind of food intervention to get me to apologize?"

Trixie smiled and reached into one of the shopping bags. She pulled out a bottle of Moet champagne. "More like a celebration."

"What are we celebrating?"

"You."

"And your independence," Penny added.

I shook my head but couldn't stop the smile that tugged at the corners of my mouth.

"Carlotta and Ella wanted to come too, but Lottie had a dentist appointment and El needed to help her ma make the mozzarella for Christmas Eve dinner," Trixie told me, indicating the wives of my two other brothers.

"Come on in, then," I said. "I could use something to eat."

"And drink," Trixie said, swaying the bottle back and forth in her hands.

A few minutes later, we sat at my table.

"You never got a chance to have any of Ma's pork roast yesterday," Penny said, forking over two thick slices onto a dish. She handed it to me and passed a plastic container filled with asparagus spears. Penny handed me the heated gravy—the real kind of gravy, brown and full of mushrooms, not the red sauce. "She outdid herself, as usual. It's to die." She pressed all five fingertips to her lips and then blew them in a loud kiss.

She wasn't kidding. Ma's roasts were a family favorite and one of my five all-time most-requested of her dishes.

When we were all set to eat, Trixie glanced at Penny and then cleared her throat.

"I've been waiting for that," I said.

"Wha'?" Trixie's northern Italian heritage gifted her large, pale blue eyes in a perfect oval of a face. She widened them, and it wasn't an affectation. Trixie isn't exactly the sharpest knife in the drawer.

"That little throat thing you do that signals when you want to say something that makes you nervous."

"Get out. I don't do that?" She looked over at Penny. "Do I?"

"Yeah, ya do," Petey's wife said.

"Hmm. I never noticed."

149

"We have," Penny and I said in unison.

Trixie looked from me to Penny, then back to me. With a shrug and a slight tilt of her head, she cleared her throat again, stopped, then laughed. "Okay. I guess I do. Anyway." She turned her full attention to me. "We was talking after you left last night, and we wanted you to know how proud we are you finally stood up to Ma and Pop and your annoying, overbearing brothers."

"Those annoying, overbearing brothers are also your husbands and the fathers of your children."

Penny flapped her hand in a careless wave. "Yeah, but they're still *idioti,* and they were acting like morons."

I shrugged. "Nothing new. They all have trouble believing I have a brain and can take care of myself."

"Like Penny said." Trixie shoved a huge mushroom in her mouth and talked around it. "Morons."

"Pesce told me after I left it got kinda loud and heated."

Both of them rolled their eyes.

"It's always loud when Pop and 'Carlo start in. Both of them are such stubborn bulls," Trixie said.

"Pesce also said Ma was a little..." I waved my hand.

"Yeah." Penny nodded. "She was a little raw around the edges when we put her to bed. First time I can ever remember she didn't bellyache about having to do the dishes and put the kitchen to rights."

"The four of us did that," Trixie said.

I didn't say *wow*, but it rambled around in my head. Ma had left her daughters-in-law to clean up the kitchen, and they'd done it without being cajoled or

150

bribed to.

It was an almost-Christmas miracle on the Upper West Side.

"Anyway," Trixie said, after taking a substantial sip of her champagne, "we figured you needed to know how proud the four of us are of you. Standing up to your family is scary."

"Terrifying," Penny said.

"But you did it, and we're thrilled for you. It's been a long time coming."

I'd grown up immersed in a cloud of sweaty testosterone, the single female child at the end of long line of hot-headed boys who all thought they were the alpha in the pack. I'd always yearned for sisters, which was why I'd sought the company of my older female cousins so much when I was a kid. Girls, I'd discovered, didn't leave the toilet seat up after being in the bathroom, didn't leave their gross gym socks and shorts on the floor in the bathroom or their bedroom waiting for them to be laundered, and didn't leave the bathroom sink gunked-up with the remnants of shaved thick black beard stubble that started sprouting at the age of eleven.

My sisters-in-law were older than I was, but they treated me like I was their flesh and blood sister-from-another-mister and I loved them for it. With Chloe and Gia busy with their own husbands and kids, I hadn't had any females to chat up in a while, and I wanted and needed that connection.

"Thanks," I said as I willed my tears back.

Penny reached across the table and grabbed my hand, squeezed it.

"So," she said after darting a look at Trixie.

"Who's this Irish guy Pop was talkin' about? Did you really sleep with him the other night? Tell us everything. Where'd you meet?"

"Yeah, tell us all about him," 'Carlo's bride commanded.

So I did.

****

The next two days were so busy at the bakery with the need to get all the Christmas orders ready to go, I never left the workroom at all once I arrived in the morning. Both nights, I fell into bed close to eleven after being up and working nonstop since three a.m. Eighteen-hour days take a toll on you when you're past the age of twenty. The last time I remembered feeling this exhausted was when Angelina had been a newborn and needed to be fed every two hours.

My mother was still on her self-imposed sick leave, so that left me a man—or woman—short at the register. None of my cashiers had complained, though, probably because the fight I'd had with my parents had already been broadcast all over the bakery courtesy of Pesce.

And they say old women are miserable gossips. Nothing compared to loud, spoiled, and foul-mouthed teenage boys, that's for sure.

Wednesday flew by, and before I knew it, it was after seven o'clock. Connor had texted he'd arrive by seven thirty, so that gave me less than a half hour to make myself look somewhat respectable and presentable. Although I knew he loved the taste of my cakes, I didn't think he'd want to be kissing my hairline and inhaling confectioner's sugar or almond paste.

Connor was bringing takeout—yay!—so I didn't have to cook. I set the table with my *nonna*'s china and got down the good crystal glasses Aunt Frankie had brought back from Florence and which she'd given me for a wedding present.

Since we were staying in and I didn't have to worry about dressing for warmth, I opted for a midcalf black skirt topped with a long-sleeved red silk blouse my baking crew had given me for Christmas last year. It was as soft as a baby's bottom and fit my curves without being tight.

I glanced at myself in my bedroom mirror and twirled right and left a few times.

Festive, flirty, and comfortable. Perfect.

When was the last time I'd been this excited about seeing a guy?

Truth? Never. Married at barely eighteen, divorced at twenty-six. I was thirty-two and acting like this was my first date. But it kind of was. My first real date with a man and not a boy, anyway. My father periodically hinted that he knew a few guys who were looking to get married and wanted to meet a nice Italian girl. He'd even asked me outright if I wanted to get married again. I'd told him no, the pain of my first marriage was still too deep, but I'd really put him off because the guys he knew weren't the type of man I would look for if I was looking. Which I wasn't. Most of the men Pop associated with were nice guys, even if their professions were shady and not exactly nine to five jobs, but I wasn't in the mood to be set up by parents like this was Bologna circa 1910.

I never believed in that expression *butterflies in your stomach* until my downstairs bell rang at exactly seven thirty. If these tremors quaking around my insides were butterflies, then they numbered in the millions.

I sprinted down the staircase and let Connor in. His hands were each filled with the same kind of shopping bags Trixie and Penny had delivered their lunch with. This time the bags didn't contain my mother's leftovers, though.

He leaned in and kissed me on the lips, just a quick buss. Those butterflies were giving their wings a real workout.

"Hey, you," he said, smiling down at me.

I could have feasted off that grin for days and never known hunger.

"I hope you're hungry because I just about bought out Mangianno's."

"I knew I recognized that aroma." And I did. Mangianno's was a neighborhood favorite and where Pop and I had last had our pizza lunch together. "Penne alla vodka," I added, sniffing the air around him. "Meatballs with onions. Chicken parm. And garlic bread."

Connor's laugh had those butterflies flapping out of control now. "You know your food aromas." We started up the stairs.

"Since I order from them at least once a week, I should."

Inside my apartment, he put the bags down on the table and shrugged out of his coat. When I held out my hands, he handed it to me with his scarf and slipped out of his suit jacket. His tie was undone. The second I turned back to him after hanging everything up on the peg by my door, I was in his arms.

He didn't kiss me, just held me against him, his hands gliding up and down my back. He smelled of crisp air, a little garlic—no doubt from Mangianno's—and sandalwood soap. I melted into him. His heart beat strong and steady against my ear, and the sigh that broke through his lips was filled with contentment.

"You feel…good," he said after a few moments.

I pulled back to find his eyes closed, a ghost of a smile crossing his lips.

He looked tired. Wonderful, but those little lines fanning out from the corners of his eyes were etched deeper than the last time I'd seen him.

"Is everything okay?"

He opened his eyes, and his smile grew when he looked down at me. "It is now."

He covered my mouth with his own, and I sensed all the fatigue I'd seen on his face ooze away.

How was it possible to understand this man's emotions so well when I barely knew him? It was weird, I'll admit, but it was as if I'd been expecting him to show up in my life, had always been waiting for him to. As if I knew in the deep recesses of my heart and mind he would come to me one day.

Like I said, weird.

Connor deepened the kiss, and I forgot about everything weird or otherwise.

After a few moments, the sound of his stomach rumbling filled my kitchen.

I pulled back, laughing. "Someone's hungry, and it isn't only me."

He cupped my face in his warm hands and kissed the tip of my nose.

"I was in meetings all day with clients and never had a chance to stop for lunch."

I slid out of his arms. "I've been working since

three this morning and only took about five minutes at lunch to wolf down a scone. I'm hungry, too."

"Well, then, let's eat."

I unpacked the shopping bags while he opened the wine he'd brought.

"I figured you liked red," he said, showing me the bottle.

"I'm Italian." I lifted my shoulders and hands. "I like all wine as long as it's good."

"A girl after my own heart."

Now, didn't that sound wonderful?

I divided the dishes he'd brought so we could share everything.

"You seem tired," I said as we started eating.

"It's been busy at work. My assistant is still out on maternity leave and before she left, she'd booked a bunch of new client meets. Taking on new work right before the holidays is tough, especially when some of those clients want to get their software up and running before December 31."

"What happens on that date? I mean, other than it's New Year's Eve?"

"New corporate tax laws take effect on January 1, so some companies need to change or update their sites in order to take advantage of this year's tax breaks."

"Sounds complicated. And busy."

"It is. And both clients today wanted to get everything done in the next ten days, which is ridiculous."

"Can your company do it?"

He nodded as he swallowed some penne. "Yeah, but it means some of my guys will be working right up until midnight Christmas Eve and then starting right back again on the twenty-sixth. Me included."

"Technology waits for no man. Or holiday," I said.

"Truth."

I bit into a gigantic meatball, closed my eyes, and let the melded flavors of ripe, juicy tomatoes, pungent onions, garlic, and fresh oregano infused into the meat dance on my tongue. Mangianno's was the only Italian-style restaurant where the food tasted almost as good as Ma's home cooking.

"*Gesu*. This is so good."

I swiped at a glob of sauce from the corner of my mouth with my finger, and when I opened my eyes, I found Connor's gaze lasered on me. His fork was suspended in the air from his hand, and his eyes had gone to half mast. If the heat that swirled around in them wasn't enough to get those butterflies migrating again, then the heightened color in his cheeks and the way he dragged his tongue across his bottom lip as he regarded me did the trick.

For a moment I sat, hypnotized. My mouth went as dry as over-floured biscuits, and I could hear my heartbeat pounding in my temples. A tiny gasp broke through my lips when he reached across the table, pulled my free hand to his mouth, and then licked the sauce from my finger.

Mamma mia!

Connor's tongue sliding along my finger was the most delicious, erotic sensation I ever remembered experiencing. My thighs pressed together, little flares of heat shooting flames low in my belly. Suddenly, like my brothers when they were kids, I couldn't sit still. I started squirming in my chair, my bottom shifting across the cushioned seat.

"I don't know what tastes better," Connor said, his voice hushed and raw with need. "Mangianno's sauce, or..."

I gulped. "Or?"

Those clouds in his eyes turned stormy, dark, and wild. I could feel the tempest swirling within him, begging to be unleashed.

"You."

In the time it took me to inhale, Connor stood and yanked me up with him. Right before his lips pressed against mine again, he said, "I don't want to talk about business anymore, Regina."

Before I could say, "Okay," he captured my lips with his own.

So many times in my life circumstances and situations have overwhelmed me to the point where I simply couldn't think rationally. All I could do was react. The terrifying moment the pregnancy-test stick read positive; the first time they put Angelina in my arms; the moment the doctor verified her diagnosis; at my *nonna*'s burial when my mother collapsed with grief at the loss of her beloved mother. All those times, my brain shut down and my instincts took over.

This was one of those times.

I couldn't have put a rational thought together if I'd been promised ten million dollars, a trip around the world, or to see Angie one more time.

Connor claimed my mouth as his own. Simply put, he owned it. And me.

I don't remember how we got there, but we were on my couch and I was straddling him. With my hands fisted in his hair and his wound around my back and waist, we devoured one another. Forget Mangianno's and my mother's amazing food. Connor Gilhooly tasted better than anything, anyone, could ever cook.

Way better. And that's saying something because I'm Italian and we do love our food.

"I've been thinking about this for days," he said, skimming kisses down my jaw. "Kissing you again, holding you. Just knowing I was going to see you tonight got me through the hellish workdays."

I bit down on his earlobe, and a shudder sliced through him.

"I have, too," I admitted.

"*God*, Regina..." He tilted his head to the side when I nuzzled his neck. "Do you have any idea how much I want you?"

Oh, I had a fairly good idea since I was sitting right on top of the proof.

And by proof, I mean...well, *you know.*

I pulled back and stared down at him. His perfect hair was sticking out at all angles, courtesy of my eager fingers. His lips were wet and swollen and flushed from our vigorous kissing, and his eyes, *mio Dio,* his eyes. The clouds had turned to smoldering smoke hot enough to singe, and believe me when I say I craved the burn.

"Probably as much as I want you," I told him. I dragged my finger across his bottom lip.

The hands on my waist stilled. The smoke deepened, fire igniting his eyes.

"Regina?"

I bent and placed a soft kiss on his hard, firm mouth.

"Do you mean that?"

I nodded. "Make love to me, Connor. I want you to, so much."

"You're sure? I know you haven't been with anyone since your husband, but are you sure? I don't want to take advantage. If this is too much, too soon—"

I silenced him with another kiss. "You're not, and it isn't. I want to." I shook my head and chuckled. "So much, so."

Connor trailed a finger across my face. I eased back and slid off his lap to stand in front of him. Taking both of his hands, I tugged him up.

His brows pulled together as he stared down at me.

"This couch is as old as I am," I said, walking backward, taking him with me. "And it's noisy. Distractingly so." I stopped and rose up on my toes to kiss his gorgeous mouth. "My bed is quieter," I said, moving again. I gave him another kiss. A kiss that left no doubt about what I wanted.

Him.

Without another word, he bundled me up in his arms again and carried me into my bedroom. I'd left the bedside light on when I'd gotten dressed, so its soft glow gave him enough light to see where he was going.

When he bumped into the bed frame, he stopped and set me down on my feet, keeping his hands around me, keeping me close.

With my eyes locked on his, I began to undo my blouse. Connor stopped me after the first button slid open.

"Let me," he said. "Please."

I couldn't help the grin that grew on my face. He met it with one if his own when I said, "Well, since you asked so politely."

His fingers, long, strong, and firm, set about the task, his knuckles brushing against my skin with each easy slide of a button from its hold. When the last fastening was undone, he splayed the sides open and rested his hands on my waist.

I'd had the good luck—and not sexy forethought—to don a red lace bra and matching panties when I'd dressed earlier. The way Connor's pupils dilated, obliterating all the color in his eyes, when he looked down to see what was under my blouse told me he approved of the choice.

He ran the tip of his finger along the line of my breast where it rested against the top of the lace and then bent to skim his warm lips across the area he'd touched. The kiss made my nipples shoot to two hard points. They pressed against the soft material, silently begging for release. Connor answered their plea. Before I could take a breath, he slid open my bra and cupped both my now-freed breasts in his hands.

He snaked a look at me, grinned like *il Diavolo* himself, and then sucked one of my nipples between his teeth.

I think I might have blacked out for a moment when a shock of pleasure like none I'd ever felt jolted through me in one blazing blast. The teasing sound of Connor's deep chuckle brought me back to consciousness. When he moved to give the same treatment to my other breast, I arched my back and moaned so loud, I could feel my cheeks heat with embarrassment. I wasn't a groaner in the bedroom. At least I'd never been one with Johnny.

All bets were off with this man.

My knees started to clang together with each nip and suck of my distended nipples in his mouth. Shards of bright light burst behind my eyes as each tiny tug shredded nerve endings all the way straight down to the soles of my feet. I fisted Connor's hair between my fingers in a feeble attempt to remain upright.

The overwhelming need to feel his skin against mine had me tugging his shirt from the waistband of his pants and slipping my fingers under the material. How a man who worked at a desk everyday could have such a well-defined six-pack was beyond me. My hands snaked up and across the solid, well-honed trench and groove of muscles, passed rock-hard pecs, his own nipples standing upright at attention as I skimmed over them. In a move only guys can do effectively, Connor yanked his shirt over his head with one hand and just like that we were skin to skin, exactly what I wanted.

The feel of him against my hands had been impressive, but bearing witness to all his glorious flesh was intoxicating.

"You're beautiful," I told him while my hands stroked and caressed.

"You're the one who's beautiful, Regina," he whispered against my neck as he pulled me up into a hug. His breath released on a long, full sigh.

I pressed myself flat against him and wound my arms up and around his neck. Emotions rocked through me, tears unexpectedly burning the corners of my eyes.

"What's wrong?" he asked, pulling back to look down at me.

"N-nothing. I'm just…" I shrugged.

"Shh." He kissed my temple, my ear, my jaw. "It's okay," he whispered. "We don't have to do this if you're not ready."

"No, it's not that." I peered up at him through the tears. "I am. I want to. I just…I've never…" I stopped, rolled my eyes, then took a breath. "I'm getting stuck in my head. Overthinking. It's been a long time since I've done this. I feel like I don't know what to do, how to do it. I don't want to ruin this."

His face cleared, and that wicked grin that made my girly bits quiver bloomed across his face once again.

"Not gonna happen," he said. "Even if we stop right now nothing is going to be ruined between us. Do you believe me?"

The truth was written in his eyes.

He swiped his thumbs across my cheeks, drying the trickle of my tears. The gesture was so gentle, so caring, I felt a little foolish for being so worried.

I nodded.

"Good." He kissed my nose. "Now, where were we? Oh, that's right." He slid his hand down my back, under the waistband of my skirt, and cupped my butt. A quick tug and I was flat against him again. "Right here."

In between kisses that almost drove me off the edge of reason, we shucked the rest of our clothes. I tugged the blanket back, and then Connor lifted and placed me down on the bed, settling himself next to me.

His fingers flittered along my breasts, down my tummy, to the top of my thighs as we kissed.

"I need to find something out," he said suddenly, shifting back on his knees with his hands resting on his thighs. His powerful, naked thighs.

I rose up on my elbows. "What?"

"Something I've been wondering about."

He slid his hands between my legs, separating them and then clutched a hand under each one. In this position, I was completely exposed and opened to his view. Feeling self-conscious and vulnerable, I tried to cover myself with my hands.

"Don't do that," he commanded softly. "Don't hide yourself from me, Regina. Ever."

A flush sluiced down my entire body. Connor sucked in a breath.

"*Jesus*. You really are the most gorgeous woman I've ever seen," he said. Right then and there, my entire body relaxed.

I swallowed the lump in the back of my throat. "What is it you've been wondering?"

He cocked his head to one side, narrowed his eyes a hair. "If you taste as good as the things you bake."

Before I could ask what he meant, he showed me.

Gesu, did he show me.

His head disappeared between the thighs he held open in his hands. Heat—penetrating, scorching heat—exploded through me as his tongue dove straight into my core, pulled out, then did it again.

And again.

I consider myself knowledgeable about my body, how it works, what causes it pain or gives it pleasure. I've been married, after all. I've had sex, even delivered a baby.

The reality of my actual knowledge was so far removed from what I thought I knew, I would have laughed out loud at my ignorance if I hadn't been in the throes of a sexual experience that was by far the best thing that had ever happened to me. Or my body.

Connor's tongue took me on a wild and wicked ride—a ride I never wanted to get off. The man knew what he was doing when it came to giving a woman pleasure, that was for sure. Just when I thought it couldn't get any better, that I couldn't feel anything more delightful or amazing, he slipped two fingers inside me. How it's possible I didn't burst into flames on the spot, I haven't a clue. Every nerve fiber in my body ignited, exploded, then fired again while he pumped his fingers in and out of me. My back arched, lifting my hips straight off the bed as I came, his name screaming from my lips. I'd think later about being mortified about how loud I was.

Connor stayed with me, riding the wave of the orgasm until I drifted back down to Earth. It took a few minutes for my breathing to calm to where it didn't sound like I'd just sprinted up a desert mountain in the middle of summer.

When I was sure I was alive, my eyes drifted open to find him reclining next to me, on his side with his bent elbow holding up his head, a cocky look of self-satisfied pride on his face.

I really couldn't blame him for the hubris.

"Um, wow," I said.

Lame response, thy name is Regina.

Connor grinned and kissed the tip of my nose. "You do," he told me, replacing his lips with his index finger.

Who knew postcoital confusion was a real thing? I didn't have the energy to ask, but he must have recognized bewilderment on my face, because he clarified for me.

"*You* taste better than anything you bake."

This time the heat that colored my skin was pure gratification, not embarrassment. A burst of energy exploded within me. I shot up, pushed him flat on his back, and straddled him.

My hands pinioned his shoulders down on the bed, but I knew if he wanted to he could have me back on my butt with one flick of his wrists. "You're pretty proud of yourself right now, aren't you?"

His smirk made my own lips pull up at the corners.

"You did scream my name," he said, with a laugh tripping through him.

"Let's see if I can make you scream mine."

Where this liberated, sexually free being materialized from, I have no idea. I'd like to think she was always inside me, lurking, waiting for the right time, the right man, to make her presence known. Wherever she'd come from, the power I felt when Connor's face changed from playful to sinfully expectant with my words, made me determined to let her lead the way.

I dragged my tongue across my lips to wet them. Between my legs, Connor grew harder and longer.

Starting at that little notch at his neck, I licked him, slowly, all the way down to his flat belly, stopping to suckle his puckered nipples as he'd done to mine, across the troughs and swells of his abdominal muscles and hipbones. With each new place I touched, I moved my body downward. His stomach went concave, all the air whooshing from his lungs when I nuzzled the happy trail of inky black hair down to the apex of his thighs.

I flicked at quick look up at him to see his neck working feverishly while his gaze was glued to me.

"Let's see how good you taste," I whispered, dropping a kiss on his swollen tip. His gasp made me smile. "Of course, I do have a bit of a sweet tooth, being a baker and all."

Whatever he'd been about to say in response came out as a guttural groan when I took him—all the delicious length of him—into my mouth. He flung his head back, his neck bobbing as he swallowed. I scratched my fingernails along his base, rewarded when his hips jumped nearly as high as mine had.

As he had to me, I pleasured him with my hand and mouth.

"Stop," he commanded on a gasp as he lifted his torso from the pillow.

I obeyed but kept my hand fisted around him.

"You keep doing that"—he placed his hand over mine—"and I won't last much longer. I want to come inside you. I want to feel you against me."

He shifted our positions with impressive finesse and made a cradle for himself between my legs, his elbows bracketing my arms. With his forehead pressed against mine, he blew out a breath. "Give me a sec," he said, his eyes closed.

I pulled his head down to rest against my shoulder. His breathing was rapid and jagged, and I was the cause. There was something so incredibly powerful about that.

After a moment, he rose up on his arms and reclaimed my lips in a kiss I felt right down to my toes. Hunger quickly mated with desire, driving us both to the very brink.

I needed this man inside me. Now. I couldn't wait a moment more. I can't remember clearly, but I think I begged him. If I did, I'm not ashamed of it.

He slid from the bed with a chuckle and grabbed his wallet from his pants.

All those years ago when I'd climbed into the

backseat of Johnny's car, I'd never even thought of protection.

Fifteen years and a lifetime later and the thought hadn't crossed my mind again. Thank God Connor was more mature and responsible than Johnny—or I—had been.

As soon as he rolled the condom on, he settled back on top of me.

Effortlessly, as if he'd done it a thousand times before, he slowly slid into me. And just as effortlessly, as if I'd held him a thousand times before in just this way, my body stretched and pulled him in.

Words were no longer necessary. Our bodies took over, knowing instinctively what to do.

When he couldn't hold back any longer, Connor came in one long, hard thrust, my name breaking from his lips, as I joined him with the fall.

****

It had been a long time since I'd woken up with a body pressed next to mine.

And, holy hotness, what a body.

Connor's front was spooned against my back, his right hand lying across my waist, keeping me securely against him. After making love two more times, we'd finally drifted off long after midnight. This time Connor got to sleep *in* my bed, and not on the uncomfortable couch.

As if sensing I was awake, he nuzzled my neck, and I cuddled even closer to him, settling my butt against one very impressive erection.

His groan put a smile on my face. "I need to get downstairs, but I really don't want to move," I told him. "Ever."

His deep, raspy chuckle had me repeating myself. "Ever."

His hand slid from my waist down to my thighs, and he cupped me, slipping one finger between the folds of my sex.

On a sigh, I closed my eyes and whispered, "Ever, ever."

Ten minutes later, we were standing in my shower.

Best shower *ever.*

"Do you have any plans for tonight?" he asked when he was redressed in yesterday's clothes. His hair was still damp, and he'd finger-combed it back from his face. I'd put on my standard baking uniform of T-shirt and sweats, and we were standing in my kitchen while the kettle came to a boil.

"I've got a hot date with my account book and figuring out quarterly taxes. Why?"

He tugged me into his arms.

"Because I want to see you." He kissed the tip of my nose. "Take you out on a real date. Dinner. Maybe a movie. Think you can put off doing your taxes for the night?"

"I'd like to put off doing them for the rest of my life," I said, resting my head against his chest.

The deep sound of his laugh reverberated through me.

"Dinner and a movie sounds like Heaven. I can't remember the last time I was in an actual movie theater."

"Good. It's a date then."

He pulled back and kissed me quick on the lips. His breath fanned out over me in a long, warm sigh that made me consider calling in sick and spending the day in bed.

With Connor next to me.

"I really hate leaving you," he said. "I wish…"

"What?"

He shook his head and rested his chin on the top of my head.

The sound of the apartment buzzer blared, followed by someone banging on the door.

"Regina Maria, I know you're home. Open up. I ain't got my key, and we need to talk."

Pop.

"*Santa Maria.* You've got to be kidding me," I wailed. "I swear he's got some kind of nanny cam hidden in here, because his timing is too perfect for coincidence."

Connor's light laugh shook his shoulders.

"I feel like we've been here before," he said.

I stormed across the room, unshot the bolt from the door, and slammed it open. Barring his entry, I stood squarely in the center of the doorway.

"What are you doing here, Pop?"

"Watch your tone, little girl."

Thirty-two years old and he still calls me little girl and chastises me like I'm five.

Even though I was blocking the doorway, Pop didn't get the hint. Or if he did, he chose to ignore it.

"Move," he said, brushing his hand over my arm. "I need to come in 'cause I got something to say to ya."

I tried to grab his arm to prevent him from entering, but here's the thing: my father is built like a truck. As I've said, I've never really known what he does for an actual living, but whatever it is it's kept him in the shape of a toned and muscular forty-year-old. My attempt at stopping him in his tracks was beyond a total attempt at frustration.

Pop barreled into my apartment and then crashed to a stop when he saw Connor standing in the middle of the living room.

"Mr. San Valentino. Nice to see you again."

"Irish. Just the guy I came here to talk to my daughter about."

"Oh?" I asked, coming to a halt in front of him, my arms crossed defiantly over my chest. "I don't think you have anything to say about Connor, Pop. That's his name, by the way. Not Irish."

Pop shot me a glare I'd seen grown men shake and quiver from when it landed on them. Not me. Since I'd grown up with that look, it didn't have the same intimidating effect.

His gaze traveled across my face then slid to the table. Our half-eaten food and wine glasses were still sitting there, abandoned the night before.

"Mangianno's?" Pop asked me.

I shrugged one shoulder, never uncrossing my arms. "So?"

"Cozy," he said, his gaze crossing to Connor. To me he added, "You sure you know what you're doing with this guy, *bellissima figlia?*"

So now I was his beautiful daughter again?

"Nothing that concerns you, Pop."

"It does if the guy is using you."

"What?" Both Connor and I cried the word. "Pop, what are you talking about? Connor isn't using me."

"Mr. San Valentino, I can assure you—"

Pop raised his hand, pointed his index finger at Connor. "Save it, Irish. I know all about you."

Connor cocked his head. "You do, huh?"

"Yeah. I do."

"What, exactly, do you think you know?"

Pop opened his overcoat and shot his hands into the front pockets of his trousers.

Rocking back on his heels, he said, "For starters, you got a web-design company going public in a few months."

Connor's eyes narrowed a bit. "That's interesting information to have since only a handful of people know about it. How did you find out?"

"I got my ways."

Oh, merda. I knew exactly what those ways were.

"Pop." My voice shook with anger and a subtle warning for him to stop whatever else he was planning to say.

"Second," Pop said, still rocking, still staring down his nose at Connor and ignoring me. "I found out a few things about you that make me concerned for my daughter and her welfare."

"I beg your pardon?"

Pop turned to face me. "What do you know about this *barbone,* Regina?"

Aside from the fact that I was in love with him, not an awful lot. But there was no way I was saying that out loud. What I did know was enough for me.

"Pop, what is all this about?" I asked instead, calling up the old San Valentino diversion tactic my cousins taught me.

My father slanted a glance at Connor then back to me. "He tell ya he's got a side piece?"

"What?"

"While you've been here eating dinner and doing

God knows what else, he's got another girl, waiting for him to come home. Only he can't 'cause he's with you." He turned to Connor. "I don't like that you're two-timing my little girl. I don't stand for that kinda crap in my family."

Connor's eyes widened to the size of my to-die-for moon pies. "Not that it's any of your business, sir, but I'm not involved with anyone but your daughter. I don't have any other girlfriends, or side pieces, as you call them."

Awww. My little Italian girl heart fluttered when he said that. All too quickly that warm fuzzy feeling was shot down by Pop.

"Oh, no?"

"No. I can assure you of that."

Pop turned back to me. "So you can add liar to the other reasons he's no good for you, Regina."

"Excuse me." Connor's cheeks turned crimson, while his mouth pulled down in the corners.

"Pop, stop it. You're way outta line here. I think you should leave." I grabbed his arm, but he shook me off.

"You don't believe me?" he asked me, then Connor, "The name Lisa DeBenedetto mean anything to you?"

For a split second, Connor's eyes went wide, then turned to slits, rage coursing through them.

"See?" Pop pointed at him but spoke to me. "Proof."

"How do you know her name?" Connor asked.

Okay, that wasn't exactly the response I wanted to hear.

"I got my ways. People who know how to find

things out. Things people want to keep hidden."

The dawn broke on Connor's face, and if it was possible the rage in his glare turned the color of his eyes black. "You had me investigated?"

Pop shrugged, his overcoat swaying with movement. "If that's the word you want to call it."

That's exactly what he'd done. Pop's *connections* in the information-gathering community were the stuff of legends. He always knew someone who knew a guy who could get him anything he wanted, be it tickets to a sold-out show or a brand new car at rock-bottom prices. Or information.

"You pay this DeBenedetto's monthly rent on a condo in Canarsie," Pop continued. "She drives a town car that has your name on the lease. Want me to go on?"

"You've got some nerve," Connor said, his fists balling at his sides.

"I prefer to call it protecting my interests, and Regina is my primary interest."

It didn't slip by me that Connor hadn't denied my father's allegations. A flash of the conversation I'd had with his mother at the fundraiser shot to the front of my brain. She'd told me Connor was her only child, but he'd told me he'd lost his younger brother to cancer.

Was that a lie?

"Connor." I moved next to him and laid a hand on his arm. Anger vibrated under my touch. "Please. Do you know this girl that Pop's talking about?"

"Your father had me investigated like I was a thug, and that's the question you ask? I can't believe you'd condone this kind of behavior from him. From anyone. Who does that?"

"I don't hear you denying it," Pop said.

I didn't either, and that was…troubling. Ten minutes ago, I'd had mind-blowing sex with him in the shower, trusting him with my body and my love. Right now I was doubting everything I did know about him, and again, it was little more than his name.

My hesitation at his question didn't go over well. Connor's nostrils flared, and he shook his head. With a glance at my father, he stalked to where I'd hung up his coat the night before.

"Connor, please." I followed him, unease clutching my insides.

"You know, Regina—" He turned toward me while he shrugged into his suit jacket. "I thought we had something, the two of us. I thought you were feeling the same things I was—"

"I was. I am."

"I find that hard to believe, since I see doubt running all over your face. I'm sorry, but I think I should go."

"Don't let the door hit your ass on the way out," Pop said.

While he buttoned his coat, he faced my father. "Not that it's any of your business," he said in a voice that could cut glass, "but Lisa DeBenedetto is my mother."

"No, she isn't," I said before I could stop myself. "I met your mother the other night at the fundraiser. You introduced us. Her name's…Molly."

Connor slid his gloves on and leveled a heated glare at me. "Lisa is my biological mother. She gave me up for adoption when I was three days old. Molly and Angus Gilhooly adopted me and raised me as theirs. I pay the rent on her condo and the lease on her car because she's divorced and has been going through some financial hard times because of it." He shot his coat sleeves and, to my father, asked, "How'd your investigator miss that?"

Then he was out the door, leaving me open-mouthed and staring after him. The silence in my apartment was broken only by the sound of the downstairs door slamming shut.

I turned around to face my father and did something I hadn't done in six years. I collapsed into his arms.

Chapter 9

Regina's tips for surviving in a big Italian family:
9. Holidays are for family, no matter what.

After Angelina died, I wasn't able to function for months. Johnny was no help since he spent his days drinking at the local bar and then passing out in the car in front of our apartment. My parents moved me back into my old bedroom so they could take care of me. When I was finally able to join the living again, Ma told me I needed to do something with my life that would get my mind off my loss. I needed to snap out of my sorrow and move forward. The British royal family's stiff upper lip's got nothing on an old-world Italian family's *suck it up and move on* mentality.

Nothing.

Even though women wear head-to-toe black for decades as a way of remembrance of husbands who have died, they still soldier on.

So suck it up, I did. I'd enrolled in baking school and then worked endlessly to occupy my mind.

The morning after Connor walked out my door and out of my life, I cried until I had no tears left, and then Pop put me to bed for the day. I slept without moving and was up at my usual three a.m., the next morning, dressed and downstairs at the bakery. My hands rolled endless batches of dough on autopilot so my mind could simply shut down and not think about what had happened. Without a thought to what I was doing, I decorated six custom cakes, instinctively and mechanically moving through the process. Not surprising, I made no mistakes. My hands knew what do without my brain instructing them through the process.

My mother had finally gotten over her self-imposed sick leave and showed up bright and early at six a.m., ready to work as usual. Nothing was said about my outburst at dinner nor what had happened the day before, even though I knew without a doubt Pop had given her a full report. She came into the bakery, hung her coat up on the rack, and then walked over to me. Without a word, she pulled me into her meaty arms and squeezed. I'll admit this freely: I clung to her like I had as a child when I needed to be comforted. This little powerhouse of a woman drove me crazy sometimes, but she was my rock. I don't know how I would have survived after Angelina's death if it hadn't been for her unceasing love and comfort.

She pulled back, stared at my face, then, pursing her lips, gave me a perfunctory nod and went to work.

I skipped lunch and dinner, taking only a bathroom break the entire day. I fell into bed at nine and was up again at three. I did the same thing every day until Christmas Eve. There had been no word from Connor, no texts, no emails. *Niente.* Nothing. I really hadn't expected him to get in touch with me. Why would he? My father had done the unthinkable and had him investigated. His reasons may have seemed sound and righteous to him, but I could understand how Connor didn't see it that way. Privacy is a big issue in industry, and as the owner of a tech company, I imagine Connor felt a little, well, *violated* would be the best word, about how Pop came into his information. I was still upset with how my father had handled the situation, but I was more disgusted with myself.

I hadn't trusted Connor, and he'd known it. I should have. Despite my father's information, Connor had never shown me anything but kindness, had never lied to me like Pop suggested.

Suggested, Hell. He'd come right out and accused him of it. That was unforgivable, especially since Pop had been proven wrong.

Adopted. The thought had never crossed my mind. With hindsight, I should have suspected something along those lines. From the first time I'd met him, his coloring was in opposition to his surname. Add in the fact he casually threw out phrases and expressions someone of Irish American descent wouldn't necessarily use, and that added to the truth of his birth.

I'd been worried my family would never accept him as someone I wanted in my life simply because of his heritage. In fact, if our relationship hadn't gone ass-over-head due to Pop's interference, Connor would be the perfect guy for me, since he was, after all, of Italian descent, a fact so important to my parents.

With a huge sigh, I shut the lights to the workroom and removed my apron.

Oh, well. None of that mattered now. Connor may be the perfect guy for me, but I imagined he didn't think the same of me or my family.

I always close the bakery by three p.m. on Christmas Eve so everyone can get home and get an early start on dinners, get-togethers, and in my family's case, get ready for the food fest called *la Festa dei Sette Pesci,* the feast of the seven fishes. It's an old tradition dating back forever where families gather, cook, and eat seven differing fish courses before midnight on Christmas Eve. I used to know the folklore about the feast, or *la Vigilia*—the Vigil, as it's also called—but I'd forgotten it all somewhere along the way. I simply knew that every Christmas Eve, we gathered as a family at my parents' home and ate until we all went to midnight mass at St. Rita's.

Ma had left work at noon to get a jump on the first course, a slow-cooked octopus dish that was Pop's favorite. Me? I couldn't stand it and neither could my sisters-in-law. Routinely, they'd serve the dish but abstain from eating it, something that never failed to escape Ma's hawk-like eyesight.

This year I knew my uncle Joey and aunt Frankie were joining us for the feast since their kids were all celebrating with their own families and in-laws. Aunt Frankie liked a Christmas Day celebration more, anyway, and this way she got a break in the cooking department for once. Not that she wouldn't help Ma out, because of course she would. These women were raised in a kitchen at their own matriarch's knees. It was genetically impossible for them *not* to cook.

And thank you, Baby Jesus, for that, because it meant we always had great food.

This year, though, I wasn't in the mood for celebrating and being around my family. To know that I'd been so close to actually finding love again and then losing it in a heartbeat was too much for me, as I'd known it would be going in. Once I'd opened myself to the possibility that something could blossom and grow between Connor and I, I'd known something could also creep in and destroy it. What's that old saw? Plan for the worst and hope for the best? Yeah. Been there, done that, bought the souvenir T-shirt.

Because I was such a coward and couldn't face my mother's disapproval over the phone, I took the easy way out and sent a text.

Feeling a little under the weather from a long work week. I'm gonna stay home tonight. See you in the morning. Buon Natale. Te amo.

I hit send. Ma probably wouldn't get the message for a while since she was busy cooking, and by the time she realized I wasn't around, I'd already be in bed. I sighed and went into my kitchen. I wasn't hungry, but I knew I needed to eat something. The first thing my eyes lit on when I opened the refrigerator was the bottle of wine Connor had brought with him.

After Connor'd stormed out, my father had sat with me on the couch while I cried on his shoulder. When I had no tears left, he put me to bed and cleaned up my kitchen, putting away the leftover food and wine.

Right now, polishing off the bottle seemed like a good way to indulge my pity party. I changed into my pajamas even though it was still afternoon, grabbed the bottle and a glass, and sat down in front of the television I rarely had time to watch. A marathon session of *Housewives* was playing, and I figured it would pull me out of my own doldrums if I watched the lifestyles of the ridiculously rich and inevitably miserable for a few hours.

The first episode was almost over and my wine glass was empty when the doorbell sounded.

I glanced out the window to see 'Carlo and Trixie

standing on my doorstep. They looked up, and 'Carlo motioned for me to come down.

Merda. I really didn't want to see anyone right now, but 'Carlo gave me that annoying impatient face that reminded me so much of my father it's scary, so I gave in.

"What are you doing in your pajamas?" was the first thing my brother said when I opened the door to them.

"Merry Christmas to you, too," I said back. Trixie bussed my cheek.

"Yeah, yeah. Merry, merry." 'Carlo waved his hand in an impatient twist. "Why ain't you dressed? We need to be at Ma's in twenty minutes, and we're already late because someone took forever getting ready." He pursed his thick lips and pointed an irritated glare at his wife. She ignored him.

"I'm not going," I told them. "And why are you here?"

"Wha'da'ya mean, you're not going? We're here to drive you. Ma told me to pick you up on the way. She said she didn't want you taking a cab or the subway on Christmas Eve."

I crossed my arms over my chest and rolled my eyes. "When did she tell you that?"

He shrugged. "I don't know. A half hour ago? She texted me to swing by and get you, so go get ready. I'm hungry, and traffic is a bitch."

Typical. I'd sent my mother a text, and she'd chosen to ignore it. There was no doubt in my mind she'd seen what I'd sent and simply decided to disregard it. Unless I was admitted to the hospital for emergency surgery or kidnapped by aliens, I had no valid reason in her eyes to skip the festivities. Ignoring my request to stay home was her subliminal and manipulative mother's way of forcing me to *suck it up and move on.*

I wanted to be angry with her but couldn't summon up any acrimony. She was simply being what she always was: a good, caring, and loving mother.

Resigned, I shook my head and told them to come up and wait for me while I got ready. Since it was just family tonight, I didn't need to get made up and fixed, as Aunt Gracie would say.

After donning a bright red knee-length pullover over a plain white Henley and black leggings, I tugged my hair up into a high ponytail, brushed my teeth, and was set to go.

"You got any cookies or pies you can bring?" my brother asked when I told him I was ready.

"In the walk-in in the shop. Which do you want?"

"Both."

God bless my brother and his love of sweet things. From the displeased look Trixie tossed him, I knew 'Carlo's eating habits had been discussed many times over.

"Give me a minute."

Traffic was, as 'Carlo'd said, a bitch. It took twice as long as it usually did to make it to my parents' brownstone.

The minute I walked into the house, the noise level and the familiar warmth and comfort of my childhood home overtook me and made me glad I'd changed my mind about staying home alone.

I found my mother and Aunt Frankie in the kitchen—no surprise there—kneading dough for pasta.

My mother looked up from the butcher-block table, one eyebrow raised almost to her hairline as she ran her gaze across my face. That eyebrow proved she'd read my text. It was her silent way of saying *what were you thinking, not being with your family on a holiday?*

"Hey, Ma. Aunt Frankie." I kissed both their cheeks and got a big whiff of flour and fresh eggs. "*Buon Natale.*"

"Merry Christmas to you, too, Reggie," Frankie said.

"You brought cookies?" my mother asked, chinning the box in my hand.

I nodded. " 'Carlo begged. And then Trixie yelled at him the whole way here about his blood sugar levels."

"He went to the doctor last week for a checkup," Ma said as she rolled and pulled the dough, never messing up her rhythm. Just like I could bake in my sleep, she could make pasta for fifty in hers. "Told him he's skirtin' the line of being a diabetic. Don't know where he gets that from. No one in our family has trouble with sugar."

I kept silent on that one, knowing what a sweet tooth my brother had always had and how my mother had indulged it when he was growing up.

"Joey and Sonny's father had diabetes, remember, Urs?"

Ma nodded. "Yeah, but he never paid any attention to it." She looked over at me again. "Ate a whole cheesecake by himself every Easter before he"—she lowered her voice—"went away."

I kept silent on that one too, because family legend had it that Pop's dad had been an enforcer for the

Tricano crime mob and had died in prison—the definition of *went away*—doing a life stretch for a murder his boss, Alphonse Tricano, had ordered.

Like I said, it was mostly legend since he died before I was born. But in every legend, a little truth prevails.

"I'm sure Trixie will keep an eye on what he eats for dessert tonight," I said as I put the box on top of the refrigerator. "Can I help?"

For the next half hour, we pulled the dough into thin sheets with my mother's pasta roller and then cut the sheets into linguine for her scrumptious shrimp *Fra Diavolo*. The name, Brother Devil, comes from the spiciness of the red pepper flakes in the dish. My mother's recipe was a family favorite, and the moment the red sauce started to simmer, the kitchen smelled like Heaven on Earth. Or in this instance, Heaven on the Upper West Side of Manhattan.

I hadn't gone into the house proper yet, so I was surprised when I did to find my father absent.

"Where's Pop?" I asked Petey who was lounging in Ma's recliner, watching a football game with my other brothers and nephews scattered across the room. Uncle Joey was asleep, his mouth wide open, in Pop's lazy chair. My sisters-in-law were all in the den watching the same *Housewives* marathon I'd abandoned and drinking wine.

"He had to run out. Said he'd be back before the first course."

"When's that gonna be, Reg? I'm starving," 'Carlo said.

"You want some cheese with that whine?" I asked.

"Provolone," he said back with a grin.

I just shook my head at him and went back into the kitchen. "The natives are getting restless," I told my mother.

"They can hold their water for a few more minutes. Your father isn't back yet." She darted a look at Frankie that I couldn't decipher.

"Where'd he need to go on Christmas Eve?" I asked. "One of his friends"—I put air quotes around the word—"need something so important it couldn't wait until after the holiday?"

"Oh, he just had to go pick...something up. Last minute."

"What?"

"You'll see. Here." She handed me two loaves of garlic bread she'd taken out of the oven. "Cut these, and put them on the tables."

It dawned on me she'd just used a diversionary tactic.

While I went to table the bread, I heard the back door open and then Pop ask, "Where's Regina?"

"Here I am." I came into the kitchen, and my heart stopped. Really. Full stop; no beating; no blood going anywhere inside me.

I was able to blink, though, so I did to convince myself what I was seeing wasn't an hallucination or a mirage.

It wasn't.

Connor Gilhooly stood with his coat tossed over his arm next to my father.

Chapter 10

Regina's tips for surviving in a big Italian family: 10. Don't ever be late for dinner, and don't make anyone else late, either.

"Connor." I wasn't sure if I said it or thought it at first, but when his gorgeous mouth lifted in one corner I knew I had.

"Merry Christmas, Regina."

"What are you doing here?" I turned my attention to my father before he could answer me. "Pop. What's going on?"

For the first time in my entire life, my father wore an expression of pure embarrassment. His entire face went boiled-tomato red, and I knew it wasn't from the cold air outside smarting his skin. He ran his hand around the side of his neck to the back of his collar, cupped his nape, glanced down at the floor for a moment and then, taking a breath, back up at me.

"Regina. *Bellissima figlia.*" He stopped and bit down on his bottom lip.

"Pop?"

Now I was worried. Salvatore San Valentino didn't possess the embarrassment gene. Not once in all my thirty-two years and through all the wacky things he'd done, like renting a fleet of white stretch limousines for Petey's wedding from a guy who was arrested for grand theft auto the next day. And by renting, I don't mean he actually paid any fees for them. Or the time he got a steal-deal on six jumbo flat-screen televisions to find out after he'd gifted them to some of the family they didn't work and had been factory rejects, the real reason they'd fallen off a truck in Hoboken. Not once had he ever looked abashed, red-faced, or tongue-tied. Until this very moment.

"Let me talk to Regina, Sonny," Connor said, laying a hand on Pop's shoulder. "I'll explain everything to her."

Okay, *Sonny? Really?* What the—?

"Yeah, that's a good idea. You two go into the den. Have some privacy."

"The girls are in the den," Ma said, her lips turning downward in disapproval as she shook her head. "They're watchin' some program about rich *puttanas. Stupido.*"

"Why don't we go for a walk, Regina?" Connor said. "It's not too cold out."

"Yeah, that's a good idea," Pop said. "Get outta the house for a few minutes. Go get your coat, little girl."

When I didn't immediately move, he flapped his hands in a *get going* wave at me.

"Um." I looked over at my mother and Frankie, whose eyes were glued to Connor. "Ma?"

"Go," she said, tossing me the identical wave my father had. "We can manage without you."

Connor, who'd been standing next to my father this whole time moved toward me and said, "Come on, Regina. Walk with me." He held out his hand.

I looked at his face, down at the outstretched hand, and then back up. His eyes were calm and warm and without any hint of the anger and hurt they'd been filled with in my apartment.

"I-I'll get my coat. Just…just give me a minute."

"Take your time. I'm not going anywhere without you."

Madonna. That was a loaded statement if ever I'd heard one.

In record time, I shrugged into my coat, scarf, and hat.

Connor held the door open for me.

For a few moments, we were silent as we walked down the stoop steps. At street level, he said, "Have a preference?"

I shook my head, and he cocked his to the right.

"Let's go this way then."

Slowly, we started.

Every emotion I'd been feeling, every thought I'd been thinking for the past few days jumped to the front of my mind. I wanted to ask how he'd been? Why was he with my father? Why wasn't he with his family tonight? Then I wanted to apologize for what my father had done, for how I'd acted. So many questions and statements I wanted to make. The words in my mind wouldn't jump to my mouth, though. Nerves, anxiety, shame all pinged through me, so I stayed silent as I walked beside him.

Connor had been correct that it wasn't too cold, but I still felt chilled down to my bones as concern rushed through me. After a few steps, I gasped from the chill, and he stopped and turned to me. Without a word, he stepped close and wrapped me in his arms.

"You're cold," he said against my temple. "I'm sorry about that, but I wanted to talk with you away from, well, everyone else."

A cold spasm shivered through me, and Connor tightened his grip.

"There's…there's a coffee shop on the corner that stays open late. Even on Christmas Eve," I managed to say.

"Come on then." He pulled me with him, his arm slung around my shoulders keeping my body against his.

Once we were seated across from one another in a booth and Connor had ordered us both tea, I asked the one question I needed an answer to like I needed my next breath.

"Why did you come to the house with my father?"

In a move that was so gentle and endearing, he reached across the aged Formica table and took both my cold hands in his. As he rubbed his thumbs across my knuckles to share his warmth, he said, with a lopsided grin, "Your father is quite the character."

"That's one word for it," I said without thinking. "A nice one. I can think of others that aren't so kind."

His grin spread. "We don't have to talk about them." He let out a little sigh. "Your father came to my office this morning to see me. Demanded to see me, actually. Put the fear of God into one of the agency temps subbing for my assistant if she didn't let him."

I winced and looked down at the table. Connor squeezed my hands, forcing me to look back at him.

"Don't be embarrassed about that, Regina."

"Too late."

His eyes softened, the gray lightening to pewter. "He loves you very much. Very much. You're his *bellissima figlia. Suo cuore.* That's what he called you.

His heart."

I shook my head.

"And, because he loves you so much and doesn't want to see you hurt again, he did what he did."

"Had you investigated."

"Yeah. I'll admit, at the time I was pissed. More because he'd found out about my company than my biological mother. That news was supposed to be a secret, but like your father explained"—the corner of his mouth tipped up—"he knows a guy who knows a guy who works at the SEC and owed him a favor."

"Of course he does." I closed my eyes.

"Again, don't be embarrassed by that."

"Is this why he came to see you? To tell you that?"

"No. He came to apologize."

What? "Get out. My father doesn't know the meaning of the word."

"Believe me, he does." Our tea arrived. Connor let go of my hands, and while the waitress served us, we didn't speak. As soon as she left, he continued.

"He said he was sorry about how he'd handled the situation. He should have come to me, man to man he said, to confront me with what he'd discovered. His loyalty was to you, though, so he'd gone to tell you first. Finding me with you was a bonus."

I sipped my tea and let its heat steep through me.

"He admitted he should have confirmed who Lisa is. He trusted his guy, though, with the basic info, never delving into it any deeper. If he had, he would have found out she was my biological mother and not my side piece."

I choked a little on my tea and put my cup down. "*Gesu,*" I mumbled.

Connor's grin shot from one side of his face to the other. "Being around your father is like watching an actor in a mob movie noir."

"You've got that right."

He reached over and took my hand again.

"Anyway. He apologized and then told me what happened after I'd left. Which, by the way, I'm sorry about. The mature thing to do would have been to stick around and explain, talk it out."

"I need to apologize for myself, too, you know. You were right when you said I didn't trust you."

He nodded.

"It wasn't because of what Pop said, though, although that was some of the reason."

"What, then? Because I don't remember doing anything that would make you not trust me."

"It wasn't something you did. It was something your mother, your adoptive mother—although at the time I didn't know she was—said to me at the fundraiser that sent a little alarm bell off in my head."

His brows pinched together. "My mom? What did she say?"

"We were talking about chocolate, of all things. She said you'd always been a chocoholic even as a kid. I asked if her other son, your brother, had been one, too."

"My brother?" Confusion spilled over his features.

"Yeah. You told me you'd had a brother who died of leukemia. But she said you were her only child. She didn't have another son."

Just as quick as the confusion came, it flew, replaced by sadness and a spark of understanding. "She was right. I am their only kid. My brother Luca wasn't

192

Molly's son. He was Lisa's."

Dumbfounded, I stared at him.

After a long sip of his tea, Connor put the cup back down on the table. "Lisa had me when she was fifteen. She'd been a rebellious teenager, and her parents were ultra conservative. Wouldn't let her date or hang out with friends."

"Sounds familiar."

"Yeah, I can see that. Anyway, she found out she was pregnant, and her parents wouldn't allow her to keep her baby, so she put me up for adoption. The Gilhoolys took me into their home and their lives."

"And their hearts."

He squeezed my hand. "Thanks for saying that. Anyway. She grew up a lot after that. Started walking the straight and narrow as she calls it. Went to college, and when she was twenty-eight, she got married and had a baby girl."

"Oh."

"Yeah. Since she was married and much older, she of course, kept her. Molly and Angus had always been open about the fact I was adopted. They always gave me the option of getting in contact with Lisa if I wanted to. The adoption was an open one on both sides. As a kid I didn't want to. Too much anger, I guess, about being given away. But when I turned thirty, I thought it might be a good idea to find out why she'd let me go, so I wrote her a letter. It was to her parents' address, the only one my folks had, but her mother forwarded it to her. She wrote back immediately and we met. It was…interesting."

It was my turn to put some pressure on his hand. "And I bet as scary as Hell."

"Yeah. She told me the reason she'd placed me, how she'd thought about me every single day since she'd kissed me goodbye in the hospital. Every birthday she'd light a candle in church for me. Worry when she heard about outbreaks of chicken pox, stuff like that. Then she told me about Juliana and the little boy she'd had, Luca."

"So, a half brother and sister."

He nodded. "I went from being an only child to the oldest of three in a heartbeat. Four years ago, Lisa called me to tell me she was in the process of getting a divorce after she caught her husband cheating and that Luca was sick."

He stopped and blew out a breath. His eyes had gone misty, and my heart broke a little for him as Angelina's face crossed in front of me.

"The leukemia was widespread. All his lymph nodes were involved. They'd removed his spleen, given him chemo. He needed a bone-marrow transplant, and I got tested as a donor. Unfortunately, I wasn't a match. No one in the family was, but they got lucky and found a donor through the registry. The transplant looked like it was taking, but then it reversed and the leukemia took over again. The doctors gave him two or three months to live. Lisa was a wreck. They admitted him to Pearl's Place on a recommendation, and a few weeks later he died."

Tears fell silently down my cheeks. "I hate cancer."

"You have company," he said with a nod. "The staff had been so wonderful, I wanted to do something to give back. Nothing would bring Luca back to us, but I wanted other families with a sick kid to have the opportunity to be free from worry about bills, expenses, and care, like Lisa and her family had been, so I came up with the idea for the fundraiser."

"Mary and Sharla called you a saint. I think they're right."

"I'm not a saint, Regina. I'm just a guy who saw an opportunity to do good and took it."

"I think that's pretty saint-like."

One side of his mouth quirked up. "We have different opinions about that, so I'll let it go. Anyway." He took another hit of his tea. "I was going to tell you all this, but before I could, your father kinda beat me to it."

"In the worst possible way. Connor, I'm so sorry. Sorry for all of this. For my father's behavior, for mine. I'm not sorry he sought you out, though, and apologized. It was the right thing to do. The honorable thing."

"I can't fault your father too much about his behavior, now that I've got a little hindsight. He was simply looking out for you and your best interests. If I had a daughter like you, I'd probably do the same thing."

"I tend to think you'd do a more legal background check and not depend on guys who got their information by cracking heads and breaking kneecaps for a living."

For the first time, he laughed. A full shoulder-shaking guffaw. The sound sailed to my soul with a side stop at my heart.

"So," I said once he calmed. I wanted to ask where we go from here, but I was afraid to. The hope that all was forgiven enough for him to want to still be with me loomed large. With it was a fear now that he'd said his piece, he'd be on his way with a clear conscience. I mean, why would he want to be involved with me having firsthand knowledge about how my family worked? If he was as smart as I thought he was, he'd run for the hills to get away from all the crazy.

Did it make me a horrible person that I really hoped he wasn't that smart?

"So." He pulled both my hands into his again and worried my knuckles. The sensation shot little heated spears straight through me. When he lifted my hands to his mouth and kissed them, all the while his gaze holding mine, I felt liquid heat pool at the juncture of my thighs.

Madre di Dio. One touch from this amazing man and I was as hot as my industrial baking ovens.

"Regina."

I couldn't help it; I sighed. "I love the way my name sounds on your lips."

A devastatingly charming grin stared back at me. "How does it sound? Tell me."

For the first time in a lifetime, I laid my heart bare. My only hope was he wouldn't leave it raw and bleeding. "Like it belongs there."

Those amazing colors in his eyes shifted once again. From gunmetal to flint then an inky coal that smoldered and smoked with desire and intention.

He swallowed, his neck bobbing with the effort.

"It does," he whispered.

It was my turn to swallow.

"The other night," he said, "when we made love?"

I nodded.

"I'm glad that happened. Well, not glad." He

clarified with a chuckle when my eyes went wide. "There has to be a better word for it, but afterward I was afraid I'd moved too fast, forced you to do something you might have second thoughts about, or regret."

"Hello," I said, pulling a face. "Remember me? The girl who got pregnant on her first date ever with a boy? If that isn't the definition of fast, what is?"

He kissed my hand again.

"You were a kid then. You're a woman now. And you're the most desirable, most amazing woman I've ever known."

Okay, that made my heart sing.

"Plus you'd admitted you hadn't been with any other man since your husband, so I knew I should tread carefully with you." He leaned a little closer to me across the table, and a gentle tug on my hands brought me in tighter. In a much lower voice, a voice made for the bedroom at midnight, he said, "But that night I wanted you so much, I was willing to throw caution out the window for a chance to make love to you, to show you how I felt, how much I wanted you."

I gulped again.

"After I stormed out, I realized I'd never told you something."

"What?" I whispered.

Without blinking, without ever moving his gaze from mine, Connor shifted in closer to me and, like an unseen magnet, pulled me to him.

"I've fallen in love with you, Regina San Valentino. I know it's crazy, too fast, too…whatever. I've waited a long time to feel this way, and I can't deny what my heart is telling my head. I love you, and I can only hope you feel a little what I feel for you."

So, how do you tell the guy who basically brought you back from the emotional dead what's in your own heart? What words can express that adequately?

I didn't have a clue, so I went with the simple truth. "Way more than a little," I told him. "Way more."

One more movement and his lips were on my mine. They lingered for just a moment, then he pulled back. "I can't tell you how happy that makes me."

He paid the bill, and we began walking back toward my parents' house. It was colder than when we'd started out, the chill in the air biting and fresh. Connor draped an arm around my shoulder, pulled me close, and grabbed my hand, holding it across his midsection as we walked.

We didn't talk.

At the house, I walked up the first step and turned around to face him. From this position, I was on the same level as him, able to look him square in the eyes. Before I could say a word, he wrapped his arms around me and pulled me in. When our lips met, that feeling of contentment filtered through me once again. I skimmed my hands up his coat and over his shoulders. My gloves wouldn't let me clutch the back of his neck.

I groaned, frustrated, and murmured, "Too many clothes."

With a tiny laugh, he pulled back.

"Are you heading to your parents now?" I asked.

"No." He kissed the tip of my cold nose.

"Oh? Do you have other plans, then?"

"Yes."

Before I could ask him what those plans were, the front window above us shot open and 'Carlo's head popped out. "Regina, get in here. The food's ready, and we been waiting for you to get back so we can start. I'm starving, so get a move on."

"You're always starving," I shot back, but he'd already closed the window.

I turned back to Connor. "I'm sorry. Family." I rolled my eyes and kissed him. "When will I see you again?"

"In about one second."

"What?"

"I'm not leaving. Your father invited me to dinner."

"He what?"

Connor nodded and started walking up the steps, dragging me with him. "Part of his apology."

"You're the last-minute item he went out to bring home?" I asked remembering my mother's comment.

"Yup."

At the top of the stairs, 'Carlo opened the door. "About damn time."

"Language, GianCarlo," Ma called from behind him.

Pop came from the living room, his eyes flitting from Connor to me and then down to our joined hands. A wide smile blossomed across his weathered cheeks as he shook Connor's free hand. "*Benvenuto.* And Merry Christmas. Come in. Come in out of the cold."

Connor, God bless him, never missed a beat. He patted my father on the back and said, "*Grazie*, Sonny."

Then, Pop moved to me, bent to kiss my cheek, and whispered, "Do you like your Christmas present, *bellissima figlia?*"

It took everything in me not to say, "At least I

know it didn't fall off a truck."

Chapter 11

Regina's tips for surviving in a big Italian family:
11. Remember that with faith and family, nothing is
impossible.

One year later

"*Mamma mia,* it gets colder every December,"
Aunt Grace said as she made the sign of the cross at
Angelina's grave. "I can feel the wind shooting straight
across my nipples. Rest in peace, *piccolo angelo.*" She
turned to my mother and Aunt Frankie. "I'm heading
back to the car before I freeze my ass off. Take your
time. Our reservation isn't until one."

Ma nodded.

"We won't be but another minute," Frankie told
her sister.

The wind whipped up around us. My mother and
aunt were burrowed in their big woolen coats, scarves,
hats, and gloves in place to protect them from the cold,
but even with all that protection, I could tell they were
feeling the chill.

"She ain't wrong about the weather," Frankie said.
She, too, crossed herself and laid a hand on top of the
marble headstone. "We'll see you soon, Angie, baby.
Love you. Miss you." Then she kissed me on both
cheeks. "Make sure you don't stay out here too long,

Regina Maria."

"I won't."

"Come on, Urs. Let's get outta this wind."

Ma pulled me into a hug and held on tight. Even through the sixteen-odd layers she'd garbed herself in to ward off the cold, I felt her shoulders shake as she tried to hold back the tears.

"It's okay, Ma."

"We'll see you tonight for supper," she said, pulling back and cupping my face with her gloved fingers.

"We'll be on time, I promise."

"Bring cannolis. Your father's been asking for them, and I keep forgetting to bring them home with me. Come on," she said to her sister-in-law. "Let's go get warm."

I sat back down on the bench.

"Baby," I said to the headstone, "Nonna and the aunts are gone. It's just me and you, now. Connor went to get the car to give me a few moments alone with you, and I wanted to wait until everyone left to tell you our news. The last time we came out here was when we got married in July, remember?"

After joining my family for Christmas Eve dinner and eating every single fish course my mother made— even the octopus—Connor had accompanied us to midnight mass. The fact he'd survived the boisterous dinner, answering every question my nosy, overbearing brothers put to him about his business, his family, what kind of car he drove, and where he lived, I figured if he could survive that initiation under fire and still smile, he could survive a doomsday nuclear event. The inquiring looks and pop-eyed side-glances he got at mass from the members of my extended family didn't faze him in the least. At the back of the church, Pop introduced him to everyone as *Regina's guy* and left it at that. I was sure I'd be the number one topic of conversation around all their Christmas meal tables that day as speculation about who my guy was, what his intentions were, and every other little nosy tidbit they could gossip about danced from their lips.

Connor saw me home and, after a heart-stopping kiss at my door, spent the night in my bed instead of going back to his apartment. He brought me back to my parents' house on Christmas morning and then to his parents' home in Staten Island. It was a testament to how happy my family was for me that they didn't even balk at my leaving our family Christmas before the macaroni was served.

We were together, officially, as a couple from that day forward.

At a romantic dinner for two in his condo on Valentine's Day two short months later, he proposed. I'd baked red-velvet cupcakes for dessert, and when I'd gone to the bathroom after dinner, he'd slipped a fake ring inside one of them, then made sure I chose that one when dessert time came.

He'd placed it in the frosting and let it stick out a little so it would be noticeable. I squinted down at it, asked, "What's this?" and then licked the frosting until the ring was revealed. It was a huge fake diamond he told me he'd bribed his sister to buy at a local costume jewelry store in the King's Plaza Mall in Brooklyn. Gaudy and shiny and so tacky, it made my eyes bleed.

I loved it.

When I started to laugh, because really it was

pretty funny, he slipped out of his chair, got down on one knee, and grabbed my free hand. In his other, he held a distinctive blue box.

I stopped breathing. When he kissed my hand and grinned, my heart joined my lungs.

"Regina—"

"*Yes!*" I exploded.

Of course I'd said yes before he even got a chance to ask.

Laughing, crying, I fell on top of him, tumbling us both to the floor.

In between kisses, Connor chuckled and said, "I had this big long speech prepared about how much I love you. How I waited a long time to find you, and you're not even gonna give me a chance to tell you?"

"You can tell me every day for the rest of our lives," I said. "Or better still, show me."

We never got to eat the red-velvet cupcakes.

On July fourth weekend, we were married in St. Rita's. Father Tom performed the ceremony, and there wasn't a dry eye in the house. Connor's family—both of them, adoptive and biological—attended. The aunts, once they'd all heard the story of Connor's birth and adoption, laid siege to Lisa DeBenedetto at the reception and, in their nosy, loving way, grilled her like a steak for details. I'd overheard Aunt Frankie ask if she was seeing anybody because she knew of a couple of unmarried guys looking to find companionship and she'd be happy to set her up. I told this to Connor, who blanched, then promised me he'd warn her.

"Well, a lot has happened since then," I told my daughter. "The biggest news is that you're gonna be a big sister. Connor and I are expecting a baby sometime in April."

I placed my hand over my puffy overcoat to my stomach. Yup, this was a honeymoon baby, and we were both thrilled. Sometimes I'd find Connor staring at me, a look of such complete joy and love on his face, it brought me to tears.

Or that could be the hormones.

Anyway, he was as blissfully happy as I was when we confirmed the pregnancy. Of course we waited a few months to tell everyone. Old-world Italians corner the market on worrying. They are truly the most superstitious people on Earth and believe the worst will happen before something good does. If I'd announced the pregnancy too early, they'd all be in church daily praying that I lived through the first three months.

I'm not kidding.

Not even a tiny bit.

So, we waited until I was past that all-concerning first trimester to announce our happy news.

"Oh, Angelina, I'm so happy sometimes I have to pinch my arm to make sure I'm awake and all this is really happening. I never thought I'd get married again or be blessed with another child." I slipped off a glove to swipe at my teary eyes. "Nonna told me the other day she believes everything that's happened to me this past year has been orchestrated by you. That you're up in Heaven, looking down on me, protecting me, and making sure I find happiness again."

"I believe that," Connor said from behind me. There wasn't a speck of uncertainty in his voice. He plopped down next to me on the bench and grabbed my ungloved hand. Immediate warmth spread throughout my body at his touch.

That battalion of butterflies I'd grown accustomed to whenever he was near or touched me, fluttered like crazy inside me.

I loved him so, so much. More each day.

"I think your mother is right and this little angel"—he chinned toward the headstone—"brought us together."

He reached out and fingered the top of the headstone as Aunt Frankie had. "Thank you," he said.

Joy spread through me.

"Did you tell her our news?"

I nodded.

Connor lifted my hand and kissed it. "She'll have someone else to watch over now."

Was it any wonder I loved this man?

The wind kicked up again, and I leaned in closer for a cuddle.

There's an old Italian saying, *ama guarisce tutti i cuori rotti,* love heals all broken hearts.

Connor had come into my life exactly when I was ready to be healed from the tragedy of my past and I hadn't even known I was. His love had restored not only my heart, but my very soul.

Sitting there, with the man I loved beyond all words and the daughter who'd touched so many lives, I truly believed she was our guardian angel.

And I felt at peace.

A word about the author…

Peggy Jaeger is a contemporary romance writer who writes about strong women, the families who support them, and the men who can't live without them.

Family and food play huge roles in Peggy's stories because she believes there is nothing that holds a family structure together like sharing a meal…or two…or ten. Dotted with humor and characters that are as real as they are loving, Peggy brings all topics of daily life into her stories: life, death, sibling rivalry, illness, and the desire for everyone to find their own happily ever after.

You can visit her on her website PeggyJaeger.com